T0333418

YR DEAD

YR DEAD

Sam Sax

This edition first published in the
United Kingdom in 2024 by
Daunt Books
83 Marylebone High Street
London W1U 4QW

First published in the United States by
McSweeney's in 2024

A CIP catalogue record for this title is
available from the British Library.

ISBN 978-1-914198-86-1

Typeset by Marsha Swan
Printed and bound by TJ Books Limited,
Padstow, Cornwall

www.dauntbookspublishing.co.uk

for everyone
who's kept me
alive

my deep gratitude to you for picking up
this book. before you begin, i want to be
sure you know this novel deals with suicide.
please be sure to take care of yourself – you
and your life are more precious than words.

The world wavered and quivered and threatened to
burst into flames. It is I who am blocking the way.

VIRGINIA WOOLF

If I have to name it
all my language won't be enough—

                    allergy that shoots through the bone

                        blood turning against itself

                        queer planet spit out of its sun

            documents in the oven before the soldiers come

                    every cell wall tongue-kissing traffic

                every organ sunbathing on its ruined mattress

There's this myth I love most about fire. And even though I can remember almost everything now, I can't for the life of me recall where it's from. Maybe a book, or maybe it's buried somewhere in the blood. That's one of the few hazy bits, the origins of things – film decays as it turns in its projector. It isn't the Greek, that famous thievery, where a man's liver is eaten by an eagle only to regrow again and again. Or those other thieves the Coyote, the Beaver, the Rabbit, the Mantis, the Crow, the Dog, the Spider. It's not the giant bear who hoards the stars to keep warm against the great black blanket of the sky, then lets one fall down to earth after seeing all humanity shiver. Not lightning. Not stone. Not two cities punished for their wont of pleasure. Not three men made to walk through fire to test their faith and – Hosanna – they survive. No, it is the story of a small child who opens her mouth to sing after her home's destroyed by a great flood and when she does, instead of a song pouring out: flames.

I hear the crowd before I see it. Leaving the park behind, I make a right, and Fifth Avenue is just sitting there between skyscrapers like a father waiting up past curfew. Gucci and Prada models glare at each other from their rented billboards – two white women trapped in time inside their photoshopped faces and borrowed clothes. I mistake the crowd out front of the Apple Store for the protest before hearing the drums in the near distance and realise these people are just waiting in line for a more expensive way to tell time. To adorn their wrists in surveillance. The drums pulsing a few blocks away sound larger than they are, spreading some old and nearly forgotten language.

When I arrive, I find the protest is just a few dozen folks inside their dark jackets inside this unseasonably warm late winter day. Two people behind megaphones are attempting to scold shoppers into joining them, begging passers-by while letting them pass. Yelling over each other, turning the street into a kind of atonal dystopian sound installation. I'm wearing a red sweatshirt that reads USA and can't stop sweating inside this ironised and ironed-on country. It's impossible not to feel how small we are below these buildings, beside all this endless traffic.

A pigeon with one fucked-up foot is hobbling on the sidewalk in a loose infinity sign. When the sun hits its neck just right at least one thing is expensive and not dying.

The last time I see Edwin it's the holidays. I'm on our old block smoking a Camel Crush beneath the LED streetlights the county's just installed; all the shadows are new and unnatural, casting weird fractals across the ground. On this annual Thanksgiving trip home, junior year, everything's smaller in the worst possible way. My father looms like a religious potato bug. My old room, a shrunken cotton t-shirt.

Edwin at least still has the old pickup, and I can hear its rust wheezing around the corner before seeing him pull up in front of his mom's house. He steps out with a grimace and has a new scar on his left cheek that looks like teeth marks or a cross-section of lasagna. He nods at me, as if he's trying to remember my name. I watch in real time as he fails to place me in a time and place.

Hey, he nods my way, and I nod back *Hi*, hiding my silver-painted nails in my pocket. *How you been?* I ask. *Yup*, he replies. Then walks away forever. I bite down and my mouth floods with menthol.

1st Degree (superficial):

At ten, I try surprising my parents with breakfast. Light the cardboard match and watch gas eat the whole book of matches, crafting a strange living flower there on the stove. The bloom quick-changes the skin on my right hand, white and frothing. It's moments later I feel the pain, like a dozen crows trying to argue their way out of me. I try to scream but it's just crows streaming out of my mouth.

Dad takes me to the ER, where a syringe lowers me into a dull synthetic quiet. Through the bandages, and the nurses, and the medicines, he calls it a lesson. Says, this pain means I'll never do it again. I nod my head and the many crows nod along in silent bewilderment. We get ice-cream, mint chocolate chip, but only after we've all stopped crying.

2nd Degree (partial thickness):

Twelve and smoking for the first time. Surrounded by other little dirtbag Jews after Hebrew School performing at toughness on the school playground with someone's mom's stolen pack of Winstons. We are learning to control fire, to take a burning thing inside us, and then let it go. For the hour, we become gods lording over the blacktop, talking shit about each other's mothers who we mostly adore and would die of embarrassment if they ever overheard. Temporary gods of smoke, of the surface of things, gods of nicotine breathing like little dragons in our graphic anime tees and second-hand JNCOs, in our filthy Chucks. Gods of new plagues and old locusts. Gods of being noticed. God, someone please notice me. Only, dear god, please not too closely.

3rd Degree (full thickness):

In college, we start a fire with gasoline and trash in the woods near campus. It's kind of a spell, at least it's supposed to be. We collect artifacts from the teachers we hate most, from exes who hurt us worse than we'll ever be hurt again and end the year with this little ritual. We perform a chant Ericka found on some obscure internet forum zir coven uses. Ericka's a witch, or wishes ze was, and maybe that's enough; how someone might become an 'artist' simply by saying so. Ze wears a long black cape, half-an-inch-thick black eyeliner, a black felt beret, and can't believe the rest of us don't have on the appropriate attire. We're dressed how all art-school kids dress at mid-sized research universities, shirts dumpstered from the local outlets, colours so sickly bright they perform our disaffection for us. We light the fire and watch it spread at first like a yawn and then like an infection and finally, a religion. It takes three towns' fire departments to come put it down. Three dogs die in the blaze. A bunch of woodland will never be recovered. None of us confess, but all of us carry those dogs still somewhere inside us.

Immolation:

I'm twenty-seven and looking out through a curtain of flames. Twenty-seven and always cold. A lit match burning in the darkness of this mid-day city. I'm twenty-seven and walking slowly through a city I love that's yet to love me back, watching people turn my way with expressions on their face that I've never seen before, that I'll never be able to name – not horror or awe, but something far older and strange.

ERICKA: i went to this art museum and thought of you.

EZRA: Me?!? ☺

ERICKA: there was this painting in the back gallery of this sad little jewish boy sitting in a corner in his little hat.

EZRA: Yarmulka? Shtreimel? Kashket?

ERICKA: sure. and there was like a table full of fruit behind him and a whole party, but this lil bitch looked like the apocalypse had just happened. it was wild! his face looked just like yours.

EZRA: Pics or it didn't happen.

ERICKA: he had BIG ariel energy. made it seemed like nothing would be enough for him. gizmos and gadgets aplenty.

EZRA: Cool. At least my dad's a hot sea-king! . . . Wait, that's kind of a read tho, no?

ERICKA: well, it is and isn't, lol. sad girls are gonna be sad girls no matter when they are painted. or how much fruit there is. i had just been thinking about how long it's been since i'd seen you and then there you were, trapped in old paint.

EZRA: Well, I saw something and thought of you today too.

ERICKA: u did?

EZRA: Sure. I saw a trash bag full of rats slowly rolling down the sidewalk.

ERICKA: aw that's sweet.

I can't make heads or tails of it, the goat on the corner of Union and Metropolitan. Of course, I've seen stranger things, living in this city: the Chabad men dragging a straw effigy down Myrtle Avenue cursing each other in Yiddish, the woman selling infant-sized dolls made out of her own human hair, the apartment fire at the popular Chelsea orgy – flames licking up the side of the building like the cheap wig of some messy god. But this goat, mottled grey coat with a short white beard, is just standing on the corner chewing on some long grasses that appear to materialise in his mouth as he chews. It's 7 a.m. and commuters walk past without noticing. A group of boys run by on their way to school, trailing their baseball gloves behind them like giant leather hands. The elder waitress in ancient caked-on make-up smokes outside the terrible 24-hr diner, looking deep into the distance, not about to be bothered by goats.

I pause only a moment; the twin slits of its pupils reflect back traffic, pedestrian and automobile alike, all seemingly uninterrupted by the wildlife. And though I can't be sure, it almost seems as if people are passing straight through its still body. All I've ever wanted is to belong somewhere, and all I can ever feel is how out of place I likely appear. So, in this spirit, I too walk past the goat as if it were a normal part of the landscape; I too accept what's in front of me and what is to come as I head down the subway steps. I leave behind the borough, and the animal, and that older man's fancy apartment, wearing his stolen French shirt after abandoning my own, pit- and popper-stained on his bathroom floor, knowing full well I'll never have to see any of this ever again.

Weekends we drink forties on the flatbed of Edwin's stepdad's blue pickup. Behind the 7/11 after dark, anything is possible. The we's always me, Edwin, and whatever collection of shit-heads decide to gather that particular evening. I say shitheads but mean only boys. I say boys and mean some kind of mollusc, hard-shelled with tender meat inside. We get the beer with Edwin's fake – says he's from Iowa, twenty-nine, and his newly grown moustache offers a little wink. I use the money from my allowance, even though he's got more, and we sit and drink until the police are called or we get bored.

These nights are endless, years blended into a stretch of asphalt, into Olde English bottles smashed into showers of light, into shadowboxing as our shadows cast huge kissing shapes below the parking lot's uniform sodium streetlamps. And Edwin smirks through all this like nothing could possibly touch him unless he invites it. Timid grin, fat lower lip, thick eyebrows below his midnight blue Yankees cap. At night in bed, when there is only my dark ceiling looking down at me, his face floats there, taking up the whole faux stucco surface, unnaturally big, eyes like two dimming headlights, his mouth a car door opening as if to say: *Get in queer, doesn't matter where we're going, I'm driving.*

My final year coincides with the *Helicoverpa confusa* or the *Confused moth* being wiped clean off the surface of the earth. The last moth was a spinster living beneath a stone bench in Calvary Cemetery you can see for a second crossing the Koscuiuszko Bridge out of Queens. The moth has no offspring and prefers to be left alone, so when this one dies it takes its genetic line with it. We're both the last of our families. This year is filled with bad news about the weather. News about new diseases in birds and mosquitoes. This year, I illegally sublease a basement apartment in a giant pre-war building in Queens at least four degrees from the original leaseholder and thumbtack photos of all my friends, those I've lost and the ones I haven't yet met, to the drywall. They're either Polaroids or photos I print out using an app that makes the pictures look like old school Polaroids. Outside my window is a Citgo sign I pretend is a rotating orange and blue moon. Late at night I kill the lights and look up at the men gathered below it bumming cigarettes, talking shit, listening to each other's voices, responding with their own, I laugh along with their jokes. Do my best at performing at the human ritual. Some nights I add my own humour to the darkness: Get this guys. Knock knock: this is it.

At first, all the past villages and townships come back in single charcoal lines. An outline, then a sketch. At the end of the world there is . . . In the end, the world is cream as clean paper, and then the walkways and porches shade in, shadows seep up as if the sheet of paper's been set on something wet. Then all at once: brilliant colour, colour even Chagall couldn't imagine. Realer than real, hyper-real. Everyone's face is too bright, the sky a wild cerulean. I don't know why we always think of our old countries only in sepia tones, wine-dark, all our ancestors in muted and mourning colours when it isn't true. My goodness, this deep burgundy petticoat, this pinafore in all that brutal saffron. It's only when I see it, all of us at once, all living again and in vivid focus, that I realise I'm no longer breathing.

At the last protest before my last protest, I grow nauseated by the pageantry – the photo-op signage, the three-hundred-dollar jackets with political slogans pre-sewn-in, the mind numbingly repetitive chanting. Maybe the problem is that I understand too well. This is a salve for practitioners and the easily sated. Supermarket sheet cake for the choir. We're gathered outside one of the president's many towers, a handful of barricades have been prearranged for us to march in circles inside. We are yelling in this penned-in section of fencing while traffic moves freely around us, demanding justice as business goes on undisturbed. And even as we say these same words over and over, it's clear we each have different definitions of what justice, and freedom, and power mean. What I know for sure is any word repeated enough ends up meaning nothing.

A group of friends ask me to take their picture. They're laughing until the lens is trained on them and then, behind their signs, they make serious and severe faces for the internet. One of the girls compliments my anti-cop shirt (which I bought on Amazon) but not my make-up (which I stole from Sephora). There are official cameras surveilling us. The cameras stand in for police while the actual police sip free coffee in their cruisers.

To be here is to be alone surrounded by people – at once watched and invisible. Over these two hours, we keep inquiring what democracy looks like, who owns these streets, and whether, if the people are united will they ever be defeated? The answers to me are clearly: not this, not us, we're not, and, inevitably, we will be. The demonstration ends after about the length of a movie, and everyone goes home feeling better – as if we've done something, as if something's been done.

I go home sick. Throw up my Burger King into the toilet. Check Twitter to see the protest trending for a moment, then gone.

It's happened again. This time at the small grocery store on Grand. I'm minding my business, trying to navigate the labyrinth of dry good bins and discounted plums, dodging new fathers failing to pilot their strollers and shopping carts at once. I have a red basket and am swinging its empty shell in my left hand like a small pendulum, a little metronome that keeps me grounded in the rush-hour chaos. I just wanted to pop in for something small to tide me over: bread and cheese, pre-bagged apples. But it's so busy, it now seems I've somehow committed to living here and am scared I might start getting charged rent. I'm standing in the check-out line for what might be several lifetimes before I see him. *Stupid*, I think, *stupid*, and shake my head until the produce blurs into oil paint. I go ahead and bury myself in my phone: open the grid of hungry torsos, twenty likes from some new stranger on Instagram, rearrange some candies. By the time it's my turn in line, it's clear the cashier boy both is and equally cannot be Edwin – I triple take, blink hard again, and yes, the nose is slightly different across the bridge, and he has those thick glasses that make his eyes seem bigger, almost like an insect's. He's still in his early twenties, which of course he wouldn't be now after all these years, smiling; not being dead.

In a town called Zloknovia, in what is modern-day Kaunas, there was a baby born unlike any child the town had ever seen. His hair was white as a clean sheet of paper against the dark features of his face. All the child seemed to do was eat. How sweet, *his parents first thought.* What a strange child we've got! *It was only after sucking his mother dry of milk within the first weeks that they grew concerned. She ached with the weight of being emptied too quick, and they moved him onto solid foods which he, too, devoured with abandon. One hundred mashed figs a day. Then onto root vegetables, a barrel of turnips and radishes he gummed to an ugly pulp. By his second month, he'd bankrupted the family and they began begging the surrounding towns for donations, which he promptly demolished under his appetite. Goats began disappearing from fields. Whole families of crows vanished from the sky. Upon the boy's first birthday, the region fell into a great famine. After starving themselves for a year, his parents, not knowing what else to do, sent their boy on a ship to America, and it is unclear whether he made it or not.*

Even our most direct family line is split like a tree with a vast underground root system. One living organism of quaking aspen in Utah, for instance, stretches out across 108 acres. Each trunk represents a whole life. You can trace your finger across the knotted roots and pass through different worlds. Most of my dad's family lore ends a half a century ago with a drunk, so he invents for me odd, older folktales. But if you do the simple math, just four generations back requires sixteen different people who suffered and laughed and made love out of nothing. They fled Russia, Poland, Yemen, Lithuania, and then there were thirty-two. On paper at least, when we left Egypt, there would have been tens of millions, though inbreeding and genocide throw a wrench in the gears of that math. According to biblical testimony, which is always to be trusted, it was 603,550 Jews who fled to wander the desert, which outside a miracle, could never support that much life. But what else is life? Besides blood, what ties us? Sometimes miracle is just another word for naming precisely what already exists. Thus, the villages and cities are many trees and many of them are gone, felled by time and fire, but the root system spread across Yiddishland and Palestine and Egypt and France and Brazil and Argentina and here in America.

When at last I die, my xylem floods with all these stories at once and I'm so full I break into scripture, into sweat, into four unique seasons.

I'm wearing a sweatshirt that says USA. It's red and the text across the chest is blue and white. I buy it off a street vendor, and even though it's only $9.95, I offer him the whole contents of my wallet. Nod my head up and down at his look of surprise. I unbutton that man's expensive shirt with its elegant French cuffs and stand there a moment, shirtless on the street. No one looks twice. I try folding the garment neatly but it keeps catching the wind so instead just lay it on top of a trashcan in case anyone else might want it. I watch it fill and deflate as if a line of ghosts is passing through it. It's February, and the weather is in terrible heat. Central Park's spilling over with families like a net filled with some species of iridescent fish. The light is light but not enough. I lift the sweatshirt over my head and put my arms through it how you'd dress a child. For a moment, my whole head is under the cheap garment, and it's almost as if I'm in a different world – a place where nothing is hurt, just a head moving slow through its red cloth portal – and maybe on the other side we'll find a country safe and orderly, perfectly formed as an egg. But my head emerges through the hole, my arms slide through the sleeves, and I'm still here. Midtown, with all these two-legged fishes moving around me, staring into their phones. Tourists ordering hotdogs and snapping selfies in front of Bergdorf Goodman. People in athleisure barking into the same blue-glowing angler headphones. The shops thrive as the world burns, selling expensive nothing: Swarovski crystal chandeliers, computer wristwatches, designer pig leather hats. I can hear the drums in the near distance. I can feel the accelerant, heaving and sloshing, at the bottom of my bag.

Some nights, before bed, Dad reads to me. When the stories don't come out of his own head, invented folktales from some made-up country where boys fall into wells or eat the sky, he'll read from a book of poems. Cavafy maybe, or Dickinson, Brooks, Hall, or Hughes. He studied English in graduate school and can recite whole books almost by heart. The ones he likes best these days are by men whose wives left how Mom did, he says, due to *a failure of machinery*. The wives were always more talented and beautiful than the husbands who lived on to mourn them in letters. One book, written by Hughes, follows a crow across its implausibly dark mythology. One by Hall sobs forever inside a hospital room. Another by Gilbert pulls at the lost strand of the dead woman's hair from the base of a houseplant. These books are ugly as they are incomplete. Dad says writing them helped these men through all that grieving and we all need something like that to pour our sadnesses into. Our own little books, or boxes, or birds. *We haven't found ours yet*, he says, *but we've got to keep looking*. You don't write a book to replace a mother, but to fill in her absence. I don't really understand what he means, she isn't dead like those other women, just gone off and chose something different. Then again, I don't understand what the poems mean either but love the strangeness of the language, how they defy sense and roil in a dark pleasure there in the air between us, as he reads:

> no opera, not liturgy, no rescue

and

> inside the world of the burning / car there is still
> language

and

> all the birds close their eyes and wings to god at once

and

> let me eat and thus become / the light

Shortly after Mom leaves, Dad starts calling me Boychik. The name sticks like a name. Like feathers to a name.

I imagine the major media outlets will do their best to suppress the images of me. But of course, every American at this time has little eyes in their pockets. Little eyes that can record, or capture a moment in time, and upload it to the cloud where immediately it'll take off like a carnivorous fungus.

At first, every social media platform will take the video down, claiming the need to protect children. Then they'll add a content warning. Then there will be no barrier at all. And then no one will care.

When the first official images are released in the *New York Post*, I'll look like something from a movie – how someone's lit on fire in a movie. As if I'm wearing protective gear, as if I were a thing with a double, being paid to smile even while being eaten alive.

Dad comes to the black hat and coat late in life. It's a slow transformation – like watching a wild fern adjust to its small new planter, the roots curling into themselves, leaves yellowing out and begging for more sun. While Mom was still here, he never had any need for a proper Old Testament God. Didn't need to dress up like some cosplaying shtetl Lithuanian, just wore normal Dad clothes, told normal Dad jokes, worked his normal Dad job teaching English at John Jay Senior. His parents hated the backwards places they'd come from and would say as much, scoffing into their cocktails; rolling their eyes at any mention of Russia or Romania. They had no interest in synagogue besides the outfits they'd wear to services a few times a year, besides the good gossip that always flowed along with the bad wine.

Dad didn't have a use for it either; that is, until he did. Well before he moved himself in with those men into that bizarre complex they call a shul, we used to go to temple and laugh at the spectacle of it. I'd pick up a siddur and leaf through the translucent eyelid-thin pages while the service soldiered on around us, the cantor chanting away on some dour and depressing prayer that's somehow meant to be a celebration of the feeling of being alive. I'd point to an unused section of that

near-illegible alphabet, and we'd translate, whispering to each
other what it might say:

> *How many licks does it take to get to the centre of the earth?*

> *Abraham also doesn't know why this service is so damn long
> either*

> *All cats actually keep people as pets.*

> *The ice-cream spot's only open 'till 8 —*

> *Amen*

The comments below the *Post* video read:

> Jeezus what an image

> Hardly what one wants to begin the day with. Such a sad story.

> Clearly an unstable individual. What a way to go out (fire emoji)

> I wonder if he was cremated . . . ? (too soon)?_

> Shades of '68

> A man of conviction

> Videos of marvel's the human torch.

> Thinning the herd.

> Ok libs this is the new challenge, you up for it?

RIP Human Torch

Getting all hot under the collar doesn't solve anything.

Well, as the old saying goes, 'build a fire and you'll be warm for a day. Set yourself on fire, And you'll be warm for the rest of your life.'

He probably was buried deep into student loan debt and couldn't find a job to pay off his 'gender is a social construct degree'

He seemed pretty fired up about something.

You're fired. (gif attached)

Who's stuck with the medical bill? You know this loser didn't have health insurance.

The snowflake has melted. One less mentally disturbed individual walking the streets.

Take this picture down. Have you no shame? Think of his family FFS. You'll do anything to sell a freaking paper.

Darwin taking out the garbage.]

I hope the sidewalks okay

Edwin comes over with a little weed. Even though he lives just three buildings over, it's the first time he's been to the apartment or expressed any interest in hanging out at all. Dad's already gone to bed, as he always does midway through his third vodka. Edwin tells me he's going to be a cop one day, and I believe him. We smoke out of a bent and knifed coke can.

I don't exactly know why he's come. He's always made fun of me at school, him and the rest of them, talking about my shoulders, how I walk, like a sissy and all hunched over at the same time. Dad once made the mistake of calling me boychik dropping me off at school. Boy-chicken they call me now behind my back, to my back, and, in their calling, I begrudgingly become that name. But recently Edwin's started messaging me a bunch over AIM. Asks if I ever want to chill. Like any freshman, I deeply want a group of friends it's easy to be quiet with. Who can do nothing together and have that be a fulfilling way of filling the time.

We blow the smoke out of my window. It isn't quite like anything I've felt before, being high. Some kind of interface descends and blurs the world, like a paintbrush, like a laughing paintbrush. We watch the little television in my room, something where men intentionally hurt themselves doing dumb stunts over and over. A man with tattoos and weird facial hair throws himself down a staircase and Edwin laughs, so I laugh. A blindfolded man crashes a golf cart into a brick wall, and we both laugh together.

I can see him outlined through his pants. His body is pressing against his clothing like it has no respect for their utility. Out of nowhere he says, *you can suck it, if you want*. And it's only then I realise I've been staring. It's not something I'd considered before in those exact terms, my body was just drawn is all, like a curtain or a weapon. Like a bath, or a circle. But when he offers, it's like a new world snaps into place, the stories in my head suddenly remade in flesh. And before I can even put words to it, he produces himself out over his sweatpants' grey waistband, and it smells like sneakers, like the sweat in sneakers flooding all my basement senses. It's the first I've seen besides my own outside the locker room, wider, with an apostrophe-shaped birthmark just below the fat head. There's the initial taste of cortisol and the aftertaste of copper as I take him slowly between my lips. I swallow as much of him as I can take in one steady motion; and even when I begin choking, it feels like returning from being outside all day. He holds the top of my head, doesn't let me up and still his hands are somehow kind in my hair. I feel my body re-teaching itself how to breathe.

He doesn't cum. Says he won't finish in my mouth. But maybe next time, if I'm lucky. I want to be lucky so badly. I wonder what it might feel like to have his whole-body twitch and spasm beneath me like a bag filled with birds – *ew*, no – more like a boy spilling over with light – *better*. I've never felt more alone or more alive.

Bye Boy-chicken, he says slipping out the window, *Maybe I'll come back sometime.*

My breath catches in my chest like a door on a chain. *Bye,* I say to the empty second-storey window that now only holds the night, one streetlight, and some branches.

There's this myth I love most about love – although of course I don't believe it. What I actually do believe, what I know – that love is an evolutionary condition, a series of hormones released in the brain that deludes a person into building a life and network that will help propagate their genetic line. But the myth I love goes like this: In the beginning, there were two people in a garden. They had no genders and had no god. They spent their days lounging and eating fruit off trees and nothing much happened outside of that – this was the world, and they weren't cast out of anywhere. They were never cruel to each other, and they never lied. Instead they lived out their lives inside their perfect closed ecosystem, and all this mess we're living in sprouted from a different garden that was actually a prison where the people were tasked with giving all the animals names.

I'm half-conscious as I'm rushed to the hospital, the ambulance makes its way through the protest how a shark moves through shifting islands of trash and plastic. The whole time I am above myself, I can't really describe it as pain – more like a million astringent tongues are slowly lapping open my chest into a cold heat. Burnt skin, hair, and plastic have overtaken the smell of gasoline. There's an IV in my arm pumping something freezing and clear. The EMT is handsome and pale with a shaved head and holds my hand through a thin layer of latex whispering over and over, 'You're fine, kid – you're gonna to be just fine,' but his eyes are dark and empty as a well with a boy trapped at its bottom.

I close my eyes only to open them on a new country. Time's unclear as ever and I am here in the middle of it. A little synagogue somewhere. The walls ornate and kempt. The stained glass depicts one of many stories, a man preparing for the sacrifice of his child, a man in intimate entanglement with an angel, a world slowly filling with water, almost always a man. Everyone's seated and facing towards the Aron Kodesh where a cloaked and bathed figure stands reading out of a book. Everyone's clothing is handstitched. Everyone's garments are the kind people hold onto, clean, mend, and pass down to children. Every time I blink: a new synagogue. In each there is a man in robes speaking darkly. The congregants respond in Yiddish or Russian or Polish or French. Then it's the same prayer, the congregants chant the Kaddish. Each grief-filled syllable lifts up from the dirt pointing heavenward and says nothing about death. I blink and there is a wailing coming from outside the building. Blink and a brick opens the stained glass. And then another brick. And then the night pours in.

The year global temperatures break every record, we go to the January protests in shorts and t-shirts. The year they riot over opera. The year they invent the assembly line, we throw bottles at the capital. The year winter is so cold, we think time itself has slowed down just to taunt us. The year I get my first phone, I have no one to call so instead spend hours growing a snake around and around its dim yellow screen. The year they release coke again in bottles. The year I take my first drink and feel a little light go on inside me. The year we stack cabbages in boxcars and pray over soup. The year the ad executives try to sell pork to Jews. The year I live alone for the first time and realise all my furniture will outlive me. The year soldiers sit at our table to eat and will not leave. The year we flee the city. The year we flee another city. The year I work in a bookstore and visit a dozen unlike apartments to collect what's left of the dead's libraries. The year we believe there is no way out, until we uncover it.

Clearly belonging is a feeling which originates somewhere in the stomach, though its sources are fleeting and impossible to locate. Being recognised by those who live beside you is a good first step. The barista with the huge gauges and the Urkel forearm tattoo who knows me by name and every now and then gives me a free coffee. The free coffee. The old woman who's lived in my building, seemingly since it was built in 1923, who finally acknowledges my existence with a little nod that neither requires nor desires any sort of response. Clearly belonging has something to do with other people. To be seen by those around you as an expected part of the landscape. Or is it a question of comparison – to be seen as more worthy of recognition than any of the others passing through? The nod and the coffee and the sidewalk welcoming your feet. To be welcomed into a place, to hear from a hundred small voices – human, animal, and architectural – you belong here. To become made aware. To be made to bear awareness. It's several months before I even notice the stone angels on the façade of my building, and a few more before I learn this was once a home for wayward girls. Girls like me. How many of us have those angels' emptied-out eyes seen, walking in circles, waiting to be welcomed inside, looking for something to eat?

For a short time when I first move to the city I live in a punk house off the DeKalb stop with a corgi who doesn't give a fuck about anyone. Deleuze is twelve years old, unfixed, and grumpy as anything that lives long enough. His coat's always disgustingly matted, and he just lies around on the kitchen floor like a member of some inbred royal family who, unable to point to any circumstance for their depression, just growls at anyone who walks past. Ennui, we call it in humans; doggui, no one calls it in dogs. Clearly, he's had many people move in and out of his life and can only care about the ones who feed him most consistently.

Five months, I spend, living in this little room off the kitchen, a former pantry that can fit precisely one twin-sized mattress and a narrow dresser. I paint it purple imagining it might brighten and gay it up some, but it just ends up resembling a coffin. At all hours of night, I hear people singing loud and badly in the kitchen, accompanied by accordions, mandolins, and the banging of pots. On the other side, I hear drunks yelling below my window outside the bar settling something urgent and sloppy. It's not until the night when the dog acknowledges me, coming home from being out late, where he lifts his old body up off the cool tiled floor and plods my way to rub his fat filthy face against my palm, that I realise, almost pathologically, this is what I've been waiting for.

Also, that it has suddenly become time to move.

Belonging, like any other emotion, is an unreachable and fickle state of mind. Mirage and horizon – it's gone once you're inside it. Based on a thousand micro-factors that float across one's field of vision only to disappear as you approach. What changes with the streetlights. Perhaps we're always stuck in a state of longing. That we are united in this. Our only country, these united states of longing for whatever it is we don't have.

I come from a long line of cowards. Not that I'd ever say such a thing out loud, either alone or in mixed company. Instead, in my family, we say, 'We were brave enough to run', or 'We had the foresight to flee', one of the many apocalypses looming off in the near distance. How many cities have we left behind in order to go on with all this surviving? How many siblings?

Belonging, of course, also refers to what you can grab and cart with you as you leave behind the only town you've ever known or the one you were just learning to call home. Whose language you've learned as if it were your own. And in each event, what you choose to carry becomes your country.

Long before it became trendy, before you could purchase them, pre-made online in their designer-sleek packaging, I kept a *go-bag*, stored in the back of my closet behind my old sneakers. In mine always: a change of clothes, a few cans of beans and vegetables, water, my passport, a little cash, a photograph of my parents at their wedding (the one where neither of them is looking at the camera, with the foreboding mustard stain on my father's shirt), and whatever book I believe I cannot live without, that swaps out for a different novel every year or so, which should tell you all you need to know about belonging.

Maybe what it means to belong to a city is that, if it could flee –
the city, I mean – you might be one of the things it would grab
in the night to carry with it so it could remember its name.

ERICKA: you there?

EZRA: Sorta

ERICKA: i was just thinking how sad it is, that all this bullshit's going to be in our archives.

EZRA: Our what?

ERICKA: our archives.

EZRA: Huh?

ERICKA: you know . . . how archives are filled with like diaries and like sweaters and typewriters and shit?

EZRA: Idk, never been to one.

ERICKA: well, they are. i was just at one here in london looking over at john latham's papers

EZRA: *googles quickly* Omg love this dizzy bitch.

ERICKA: ya. it's filled with all these thoughtfully preserved letters and notes and some of his clothes and stuff.

EZRA: If I ever go to one, I'm gonna to eat all of the letters.

ERICKA: you'd get ARRESTED.

EZRA: Yes, but then I'd be full of secrets.

ERICKA: annnyyway, what i was thinking was how sad it is. that when we're dead, it's just going to be all this bullshit.

EZRA: Our texts?

ERICKA: ya, these are our letters students will be reading in our archives.

EZRA: Omg, Im gonna burn my phone.

ERICKA: already in the cloud. we're cooked. it just made me sad, i thought of you.

EZRA: Yr sweet. Want to start writing letters?

ERICKA: ew. absolutely not.

EZRA: You think people will want to read about us after we're dead?

ERICKA: they will for me. you can be in my archive.

EZRA: Thankgod. Glad to know I'll have a home when this is all over.

Late autumn comes on like a cold dead watch, the trees slowly strip out of their bright colours. I'm in my old room in Dad's apartment. I've been in college only two years but feel already like a wholly different bitch. I wear dark unblended eyeshadow and change my pronouns whenever anyone asks. I sleep on the couch in what is now his 'office', which he basically just uses for storage since he retired, or was fired, or whatever, from his teaching position. He's made the place hoarders-level weird. Junk piled up in ionic columns. Judaica mostly, dusty books written in dead and resurrected languages, polished ram's horns in glass cases, my parents' ketubah framed on purple imitation velvet with a big red X sharpied over it.

I open my phone and scroll through the men of this small town, through the small-town men, hoping to recognise some-one from high school, a bully maybe who's softened or saddened over the years. But everyone's icons seem to be either sunsets or abs. It's all abs and sunsets in this small town. It's mid-afternoon and the room is filled with a cold, gold light. My father's off somewhere with his weird new friends, sitting around a bottle of something dark. These men worry me. They're all frum and ugly. They speak in codes and grow large beards that smell like old fishermen's gloves, but at least he has friends.

I reach out to the sunsets in my phone, to the washboard men, hopeful. *How's it going? Hot crepuscule. Looking?* But no one messages back, just sunsets. Then, as I start to drift off, a ping from *Pending Review*: an image of a tree – I don't know what kind, some conifer, evergreen, something that refuses to lose its leaves, a stock image. The profile, similarly empty. No age. No occupation. Just distance. *Sup Boy-chiken*, the message reads, *welcome home*.

After being here for three years, I still don't have any real irl friends. Perhaps that's just the nature of living in this city? I go to meetings to try to make sense of a dying world. Melodramatic, I know, but also – whatever the meeting, I go. There's a rainbow fan of schedules stuck to the fridge under a magnet shaped like the flat round earth from space. The LGBT Resource Center holds the most interesting ones most frequently. It's housed in a remodelled church on the westside. Just around the corner is a pharmacy wedged into an ornate former bank. Everything in this city seems to be built this way, repurposed in the body of something once loved or prayed inside of. A hermit crab dragging its wrecked body from house to house. The meetings range wildly, and I learn how to be a ghost in a circle. To smile and render a surface of pleasantness. Join sub-committees and affinity groups only to be unavailable to meet in person when the time comes. There are expressly political organisations, queer and trans religious groups, addiction meetings, language learning groups, and book clubs where I pretend to have read the book. I've learned to say things like: *The arc of history bends toward* [   ], *the fragmented shape of the story suggests* [   ], *the unlikeable and unreliable narrator tells us* [   ]. There's something about being around people dedicated and working desperately toward something, anything, that makes me feel as if it's going to be alright, and if not alright, then, you know, manageable, and if not manageable, then at least something we'll endure together. So I owe them my life, these people. What's left of my life, I owe them.

I go to the protests alone and leave alone. I don't know how to introduce myself to anyone besides signing their petitions. I can't even bring myself to do the chanting. Whenever I do, all I hear is my own voice, alone next to everyone else's. Here I am singing along to the radio while the rest of the world is somehow inside the radio singing together.

When Dad sends the YouTube link, I assume it's a joke. I haven't seen him since I moved to the city. Not since my short recovery back in his apartment following that four-day stint in my college town's hospital. I hardly recognise the man there in the little white box, with his dark beard and sunglasses, his affected Yiddishisms. I hardly even recognise his voice at this point, like he came to this country on some shit boat through the torn scrim of history. My dad doesn't even speak Yiddish, his normally thick Queens accent is simply punctuated now by a few guttural and forced alien sounds. Even stranger is the part after a few minutes of sermonising, quoting Maimonides and Madonna (her Kabbalah period), where it becomes clear he's selling something, and the name: *Z'Rebs Miraculous Waters: 26 dollars a vial, to bring good tidings into your life*, floats there pixelated above his speaking face. A bit of a mouthful – could use some rebranding. While he extols the virtues of his holy product, text scrolls across the screen of the water's various uses: washes your hands, wears in your hair, waters your plants, cleans your pets, brings you to God, cleanses your Neshama, etc. etc. I call immediately and he picks up on the first ring.

Dad, what the fuck is this?

He tells me his shul's discovered a font in the woods near their new building and made the decision he would make the best spokesman. His teaching background and all. He tells me it's a great honour.

And when the fuck did you become a rabbi?

I never said I was a Rabbi and what's a Rabbi anyways? Who gets to say? You?!

Through the phone I can hear him grumble and wave his arms around like he's clearing smoke.

You don't understand Ezzie, it is a miracle. A real living miracle. I haven't felt this clear in years. I heard the voice of God in those waters. He called my name. It's a bentshung for the shul, you know? We've been struggling a bit, financially, paying our rent. Even with all our savings. Anyhow, please share this with your friends. Perhaps in your Facebook. Halevai.

I try to think of who to call – who still talks to my father and might be able to talk him down or help him return to some kind of baseline stasis – but can't think of a single person. After he gave up the apartment and moved himself into that ugly former elementary school with the rest of those men, I kind of lost track. I start to write an email to one of his old colleagues from the high school, but halfway through realise the only person left to intervene is going to be me.

The weight of the father is heavy, I think, but can't place the quote. Honour thy father, I think, and know where that one's from. But what the fuck do I know about being able to offer real care for this new lunatic? I look around my apartment – the busted-in window screen, the never-once-washed fitted sheet, the same blue mug I drink all my liquids from –

I can barely take care of myself.

So, I give up and share the link.

Dad's new friends are a bunch of fucking wack-jobs, I think, putting on another coat of black matte lipstick after deepening my electric blue eyeliner. At the same time, I'm glad, I guess, he's got people around him; I was so worried when I went off to college that he would be all alone. He met these men through the AA meetings in the synagogue basement that I wish he still went to. In the living room they're sitting around a bottle of something Russian, playing a game with what look like dominos, only the tiles here are covered in strange characters. There's a kinda stank smell about them, even through the veil of cigarette smoke, which means up close they likely smell super funky. The men are wearing old black suits and the tallest guy's got one of those fur shtreimels sitting askew on top of his head. They look like Hassids, but then again it's a Friday and one of them's blasting Kylie Minogue from a set of speakers wrapped around his neck.

What are you guys playing? I ask on my way out the door, and they all turn to me at once, almost in slow motion, a group of garden snails happening upon salt. Clearly none of them was expecting anyone else to be in the apartment.

The headphone neck guy replies, *We should really be asking what you're playing at young chazzer? Heading out of the hoiyz dressed loike that*. And they all let out a tinny laughter while Dad looks on embarrassed, like I'm the weird one here. He looks around nervously at his new friends.

Cool. I reply. Then step out the door to go meet up with Edwin, or whoever that conifer was, in the old parking lot field.

Once a week I go to Nowhere. It's a long basement on Four-teenth Street. I go to Nowhere on Tuesdays and am no one there. Ride the thirty-minute subway from my apartment to sit behind a beer or a mixed vodka drink or a slushy during the summer months and stare into my phone or at a book in my phone. I like it most when it's dead. I go to be a boy there, in my most boy drag. One *what'll it be honey?* from the husky bartender with barrettes in his hair is all I need, and that little sweetness can carry me through the week.

I love being at once a regular and irregular, both present and unknown. Acquaintanceship is next to godliness. O, to speak to people tender and fleetingly in the dark underneath crushing music, to kiss an old man in the bathroom and know you're bringing him joy, to be a good boy for once, to pretend you love his cocaine and know this is a kindness, a muscular avuncular arm over your shoulder or sliding down into the back of your jeans. Every Tuesday a new man can be a brother ignoring me from across the room. I've learned to make eyes that say more than a mouth ever could. I've learned to make my mouth a watering hole. I love meeting strangers at Nowhere, and knowing it will go nowhere, that this will likely be the only time we ever speak.

I'm lucky to have died when I did. Before I went, my primary feeling whenever anyone left was jealousy. Besides my friends, there was the highly visible cavalcade of beloved celebrities. Comedians and musicians fell, some to old age, others taken by their own hand. Leonard Cohen, Prince, Robin Williams, Carrie Fisher, David Bowie; and one by one my friends, who nobody knew – not even me, really – were commemorated by a small processional, a Facebook post, a memorial page you could visit, a few dozen torsos gasping in the privacy of their own isolated homes, a tasteful service around a machine-dug hole. Even those I was never close to in life – I felt their absence deeply. People who maybe I had sex with in private messages on Snapchat or Instagram or loved only from afar. Maybe we texted as we touched ourselves in the dark, sent each other dim photos or videos of ourselves in the far-off throes only to have our sex disappear into endless data. Knowing full well these tech companies store our gone messages, so that even after death, in some database somewhere, we are both alive and still hungry for each other. Still as close and as far apart as we ever were. And what I felt, each time I learned about their passing, wasn't grief or anger, it was envy.

When I get the news about Edwin, I go make an appointment to get a tattoo of an octopus on my stomach, the head just below the belly button, the arms crawling up and around towards my chest. It takes four hours with whoever's first available at Karma Tattoo to get just the outline in black. Their name's Xandria and while their line work leaves much to be desired, somehow the jagged asynchronous arms seem fitting for the occasion. While their needle's inside me, they ask about the tattoo and I tell them: octopi have three hearts and no backbone – like me, and they smile. I say: octopi can change colour and shape to blend into their surroundings and shoot ink when they're scared – also me, and they smile again. What I don't say, is anything about Edwin. The whole time, I manage not to cry once.

Though I'm nervous to try it, my college boyfriend and I take DMT at the cemetery. Neither of us have done it before. He tells me it's the chemical that releases in the brain when you die. Groovy, I reply. He thinks it'll bring us closer together, while I'm just hoping it might be enough to salvage the little sinking ship of our romance. He was something I'd fallen into, meaning he was interested enough and one of twenty gay boys on campus, so I went ahead and went along with it. We met at what was supposed to be an orgy in a dorm room but just ended up being six of us sitting around drinking Pabst culminating in one clumsy blow job, while a couple of us shyly jerked off sitting on sad and ancient furniture. Quinten loves the cemetery. To me it feels disrespectful, to spend time around the dead in that way, almost voyeuristic, but it's what he wants, so I guess I'll want it too. Tall and slender, with dark stringy hair, he could be one of these trees, watching over us watching over the headstones. He places the bitter powder on my tongue in the silver hour and it doesn't kick in until we're making out on a bench next to the grave of some child who died of tuberculosis a hundred years ago. It's night and the moon's like a floodlight. We're kissing and I'm slowly rubbing his cock through his jeans, when his mouth begins to open wider, which is odd – and then wider than I imagined a mouth could open, and I find myself, closed eyed and falling through the dark tube of his throat, back through time. Back before even that kid died, and all there was here was grasses. When this whole town was woodland. The trees are reaching up their dark fingers toward the cycling light then falling again across millennia, all the way back to the birth of colour, when it split from whatever solitary light source, and I branch into every body that made a body for me to be here, all of us speaking at once, all of us so hungry and fleeing somewhere. At last, we return to that one singular fig that all life sprang from with a dead wasp gasping inside, and I cry there with it for another few centuries, letting it sting my tongue again and again. I've never been more connected to another person than when I realise we're still sitting there on that cemetery bench sobbing into each other's open mouths. *Thank you Thank you Thank you*, we keep saying. We break up later that month.

In a small village formally known as Bhlikovta, men in uniforms came to tell the people their village wasn't a village anymore. The men used fire to make this point and, from out of the village, a writer was cast into the winter roads alongside the rest of his neighbours. As they walked through unending darkness, his neighbours asked him to recount their life in Bhlikovta, to build it back for them in words. They said, tell us about the creek where we used to pretend we were spawning fish, tell us about the fields where we buried our dogs. I'm a writer, the writer replied, I can't speak back to you what was as if it is, but rather can only record it for you once it is gone, to offer an isness that isn't is any more, do you understand? At this reply, his neighbours found themselves quite annoyed, wanting only their dinner tables back, the floors they birthed their children on, the places they sang in joy and in pain. They wanted the writer to write a reprieve for their suffering, to take them away from the stabbing cold in their feet. After weeks of journeying, when eventually the whole village abandoned the writer to his walking, scattering across neighbouring towns that had yet to be unpersoned, the writer sat down at a child's desk in a bombed out primary school and began writing. He recorded first all the particulars of a life in objects, no ideas, only things, pages and pages of cutlery, of scarves, and of shovels, and one by one each common noun appeared around him. After building this blueprint of his gone village, in a shaky hand, he followed with this: I did not have a home, until it was gone from me.

Things just sort of happen to me. I don't know how to say it other than that. One morning I open my eyes and I'm inside a different life. I'm working as a security guard for an old ware-house. I'm drinking in the boiler room after a fancy cocktail party. I'm boxing up a room full of a dead woman's books. I'm getting rid of my whole wardrobe and replacing it with greens and olives. I'm returning to the scene of the crime. I'm blinking like a turtle at Riis Beach lying on a towel surrounded by half-naked and dancing friends whom I love dearly and may never see again. I walk through the city and am no one until someone speaks and gives me a name. I decide where to live next when I'm invited. I attend the job interview and get hired because of an acquaintance. It's almost as if there's no continuity at all between tomorrow and what precedes it – or maybe my memory just starts me off each day fresh, not an entirely new highway, but I wake up beyond the next bend. Even when I almost married Christian, I knew it would only be for a moment, that even 'forever' is just a moment in time. With enough pressure or pleasure I can be talked into becoming almost anything, I know this. He proposes after I've moved into the studio in the basement of his parents' brown-stone and I couldn't for the life of me tell you how either of those things happened. He fucked me raw in his apartment once, and then it's four months later and he's proposing. On a knee, like he's being knighted, wearing the black romper with pineapples that always embarrasses me. There's a decoder ring in his hand that must have been some kind of joke between us I scarcely remember. I feel empty when he does it but say yes to spare myself the look on his face. He's just got a job in finance, which means he's going to be gone much of the day moving imaginary numbers around, the kind of numbers that repossess people's houses and drive up the price of baby formula. It's easy until it isn't. We order in food. He looks deeply into my eyes when he's inside me. I do my best impression of presentness to convince him he isn't just looking back into himself.

It's on television that I first see the president's tower, in reruns of *The Nanny* and *Home Alone 2: Lost in New York*. It appears for a few brief seconds before the camera takes us inside the lobby, with its salmon marble and gaudy gilded furnishings. We cut then to some meeting or other, a boardroom, leather furniture, chintzy light fixtures. It sits there on Fifth Avenue like a badly rolled blunt, dark stalagmite reaching heavenward, Babel's ugly little brother. Then it was just a dumb icon, an ugly-dark building with a hideous Stymie Extra Bold font shining like gold teeth in its mouth.

The Golden Gate Bridge is the most popular suicide destination in the United States. Every year around thirty people throw themselves from its red arms into the black waters of the bay. I wonder how they felt when they first saw it? Was there some immediate recognition – *that is where I will die* – or was it more subtle? Did it plant itself in the head like some kind of invasive vine? Did it grow there slowly over billboards and stop signs until, one morning, you get in the car and drive to California?

I can't be sure it's Edwin until I'm in the parking lot. He won't send a picture over the app but the fact he calls me *Boy-chicken* leaves me hopeful as an open window. When I arrive, he's already there behind the 7/11, and for a moment I wonder if he never left, if, for the past two years he's been sitting there, slowly smoking the same cigarette. Though when I get closer, it's clear he's lost something besides the weight; he's grown a bit more distant behind the eyes, thinner in the cheeks. Tells me he tried the military and was returned home early, but doesn't say why.

We're lying out in the bed of the truck, looking up at the few stars bright enough to make themselves visible through the pollution. Our smoke above us looks like trees when it's cut through by passing headlights. We're quiet a long time, when out of the blue smoke, he asks me to fuck him in a voice I've never heard from him before, a thin high whisper, the peeling back of electrical tape. The request takes the wind out of me but only for a second before I oblige, as I would have obliged him anything. I'm bare but don't care about it. He's on his back and it's filthy and I do my best to lift him up to a good angle. He's crying in his quiet way and looking up at nothing in the sky and I ask if he wants me to stop, but each time I ask, he slams his fist against the side of the cab, muttering for me to shut the fuck up. So I shut the fuck up and fuck him until his eyes roll back and it's clear he isn't anywhere inside his body.

After I've finished and do my best to clean myself off with a half-drunk Aquafina bottle, I light each of us one of his Newports and he seems his old self again, confident and bright after being split, glowing like a geode. On his phone, he shows me this video of an octopus caught on a security camera escaping from the aquarium. You can see in the grainy footage, one of its many arms opening the roof of its watery cage and then its amorphous body slides down the glass. On its way out, the animal snatches a fish and eats it in its lower mouth as it disappears out of the frame and into freedom. He laughs, so I do. He asks where I think the octopus is now – dead or still running?

In the early years after Mom leaves, Dad brings home stacks of paper from the school. They're filled with the dreams of his students. Every spring the living room fills with notebooks filled with dreams. Some nights, when it's late enough, I sneak down to read them. One book is filled with falling and flight – in every dream is something that flies, winged or otherwise. Another is all about running from the end of the world. Another is full of terrifying dentistry. The students love my father, call him Pop. He's teaching a unit on poetry, and wants them to turn their dreams into poems. He never asks me my dreams anymore. Never takes my dreams to school with him on paper. It's been a hard few years for all of us, is what he says when I ask.

He has a room somewhere filled with other children. Siblings I'll never meet but whose names make Dad smile when he says them. He's teaching them the books of poems he reads to me at night. So, I comb through the work of the students who call him Pop. Who must love him like their own fathers. The students are using their dreams to write imitation poems of these grieving old men, and I'm grateful when I see it. Maybe this means that I'm a part of something, that I'm connected to a story worth following, worthy of being studied by a room filled with kids who only want to learn from my father.

Mom's a poet too, though not with words, but with paints. One spring she painted the whole living room in flowers. Sunflowers mostly, but also zinnias and dahlias. They looked so real you might have thought they were breathing. The winter she left us, Dad painted it all grey. She was gone only a few days when he did it, and the whole apartment's been grey ever since. Here, in the grey room, Dad reads the dreams of his students and laughs. Bent over their pages he writes them messages and asks me to pour him another drink.

When I am a child, my parents move us from Queens to a town off the Hudson that, like them, came from money, only then the money left and what remained was just scaffolding. Ghost husk of a town. Where once-thriving industry had left the empty shells of factories perfect for exploration, for gathering and burying secrets. Suburban tract houses cowering between gutted estates, all in slow fungal decay, mould spreading its fingers across the walls of the once-grand houses.

I can tell where and when I am based on what cigarette I happen to be smoking. Always found it easier to adapt to what the person I happen to be intimate with happens to be smoking. True, too, of most interests, really; taste turns out to be mutable and multiple. Drag Race with Quentin at the campus bar. Happy-hour oysters with Malcolm. Board games with Arnold. Bad horror movies with Christian. The opera with Kristopher. And on and on. In each audience, I quickly become a new devotee, seasoned enough to roll my eyes at all the posers and imposters around me. I adapt to whatever the faces around me serve, all adept at their respective rituals of enjoyment.

Mom's Marlboro Lights I refuse on principle.

Dad's unfiltered Pall Malls you can tap out one at a time on your knee from their soft pack.

Edwin's Newports, my first of many things, including menthol, the just-brushed feeling of death.

Kevin, with the old oak taste of Lucky Strikes before they and he were both cancelled.

Gerard and his Parliaments with the recessed filter, which he told me was there to put in a little cocaine, even though I never believed him . . . about anything.

Quintin's Camel Crushes, the third best of two worlds, a transformation from ash into ash.

Ericka's Yellow American Spirits, forced into that antique cigarette holder, before ze got me smoking a pipe.

Arnold with his Kamels with a K in the fancy red pack.

Malcolm and his rollies, Samson brand, which by the end of our time together he started rolling in those little Swann filters, that would fly out of the cigarette into the back of your throat.

Kristopher and his Gauloises, of course, asshole.

Christian and his Marlboro 27s, which always taste to me like chemicals and sap, the flavour I imagine will survive us, where the taste of the natural world meets all the horror we've made here.

Depending on the year, all my friends migrate between digital spaces. I make several accounts at once with different photos and names. It's nice to visit the life of someone else for a little while. To not have to account for one's own body in time or space. To breathe differently through how you type. In this world, everyone is and isn't precisely who they say they are. Freedom untethered from history. Pleasure and companionship can take on any shape so long as you're able to imagine it. Into the deep evening, I laugh out loud from my real body with my new friends, we talk shit and tell jokes, compare notes, and send memes. We meet up on The Sims and share secrets wedged between our lies, make our avatars kiss, send nudes from the neck down, and from out of our imagined lives, share our lives.

ERICKA: this past month i fell in love with three different women named mary.

EZRA: Holy Holy! All virgins?

ERICKA: not anymore.

EZRA: L O L. Any keepers?

ERICKA: nope, i think not. here and gones. it was love for a moment and then the moment passed.

EZRA: I believe it . . . I've never been in love, what's it like?

ERICKA: liar.

EZRA: Honestly.

ERICKA: well, if you're actually asking and not being an asshole . . . it's a thing that takes over your limbs and breathing, so all-consuming you can't feel or think about anything else. like falling from a great height into another person's body.

EZRA: O, so like a possession, or addiction or something?

ERICKA: not not.

EZRA: Yeah, never felt that . . . I am engaged though!

ERICKA: like as in marriage?

EZRA: Precisely.

ERICKA: poor guy.

EZRA: Tell me about it.

I've learned his schedule. He doesn't work at the grocery store weekends or Wednesdays, so I go on Thursdays and make sure I'm in his checkout line so we can exchange pleasantries. But that's the extent of it. I bring my own tote, and every time he says something enthusiastic and goofy like, *Way to go Planeteer!* or *Rock the tote!* with a practised dweeby casual wink I'd find disgusting if he wasn't the spitting hot-ghost-image of my dead ex. One Thursday I decide to see where he lives; it's not like I have anything better to do. So I wait across the street on a bench and see him leave around 7 p.m. then follow his mustard yellow varsity jacket and slicked-back black hair down to the G Uptown and we ride the train together into Queens. He looks tired after saying the same thing all day, *have a nice day*; reluctant gatekeeper standing in the way of a few hundred people's dinner. I know it isn't him and still – I follow the rules I've learned from detective films, one car over, only looking at him in reflections through the little rectangular window between us. When we transfer at Court Square, we're waiting on the packed platform just beside each other, and my pulse picks up a bit. He looks over to me, and there's a shine of recognition, a quizzical eyebrow; he nods and I blush – *shit*. I look away and pretend to read my book, it's nonfiction about public sex by Samuel Delaney, which I'm surprised hasn't led to more anonymous sex of my own. He's in his phone until the E train comes and standing in the same car in a crush of people we head toward Jackson Heights. I can't tell whether he recognises me or if it's just that I'm hyper-attuned to every micro-expression moving across his face like weather. We're both holding onto the same metal pole, and I can feel the heat coming off his wrist, all that blood flowing just beneath the surface – realising only now why this is where people spritz perfume. At each stop, more people get on, pushing us closer together until our bodies are somehow creased against each other, his pelvis on my hip, each jolt of the train car pushing him a little harder into me. It's so packed you can't see what's happening below the torso, so I press back; I can't help it. He's not looking at me but I can feel him hard there. I wish I had more nerve endings in my ass so I could feel the outline more clearly. We stay this way until 75th where I follow him off the train. He still isn't looking at me and I'm not sure if I imagined all this – it seems as if it might have just been in my head – but once we climb the steps up into the daylight he pushes me into the doorway of a shuttered taqueria and bites my bottom lip hard, drawing a little blood. *I live around the corner*, he rasps. The light is so grey it makes all the colours pop, the green in the trees is almost unbearable. I follow him up Elmhurst, and we're quiet the whole way, but my pulse is drumming so loud inside me, he has to be able to hear it. When we walk down the steps to his basement apartment, he turns to me with his key already slid in the door and says, *My name's Christian, don't tell me yours*.

My first proper date with Christian is tea, which isn't something I've ever done – had tea with someone and have that be the whole thing. Tea has always seemed like an afterthought, what you do to make something last a little longer – a bit of nothing, hot water with leaves – that or something to soothe the stomach when you're by yourself and sick in your empty and infinite apartment. Regardless, it feels horribly adult and effete, but I affect what I hope is a demure and disaffected demeanour, like this is something I do all the time. He orders a tea that turns his water plague red, and I point to something on the menu so as not to have to embarrass myself by attempting the multisyllabic consonant-heavy name aloud. I don't realise my mistake until it's too late. At the end of the cup, I become laundry on the line caught up in an electrical storm, my skeleton vibrating on the other side of the table. I become this entirely new, very talkative and alive person, which is deeply unlike me, and I suddenly have so many questions for this man but no time to listen to his responses, with his dark hair pulled back into a tight bun, who I thought at first was Israeli but turns out to be Lebanese, which makes me triple-glad I hadn't guessed. I talk, making occasional space for his affirmations where he smiles and nods his head along. He says, *okay*, and *no!* and *uh-huh*. I go on and on about whatever bullshit: the history of the piano, Britney's conservatorship, the evolutionary rationale for scent. I apologise mid-sip on cup two, explaining I'm not normally like this, speaking all frantic, loud, and impatient – interested. And that he shouldn't expect this particular iteration of me at future teas, inquisitive and forthcoming. He smiles over the wood-stained table decoupaged with hundred-year-old news clippings – *There will be more teas?* I blush or flush with caffeine, glance down for a moment at the *Hindenburg*, the zeppelin caught in time dressed its infamous white plumage, and I smile back like an idiot, not knowing what else to say, but, *obvi*.

What follows birth is the ritual of preparing the body for bureaucracy. I remember everything now, exactly how it happened. The injections, the weighing, the measurements, the footprint, the incubator, the little white gown, the giant dilated adult pupils staring down through glass, the gloved hands, the lowered breast, the woman crying as I refused to make eye contact, the nurses and the nursing. Most people don't remember their early infancy, which is a blessing. The first few months are an agony. Imagine feeling your soft wet skull still in pieces, the brain pressed directly against the skin, imagine feeling your skull bones slowly fusing into one complete object. Imagine the world inverted, a doctor in a white coat walks upon the ceiling. Imagine how there's no language, just a collage of fractured sound, a shouting colour with neither order nor meaning, no sense to temperature, food running through you like water through a busted faucet. I am left in a room full of other infants, each in our own discrete plastic birth-coffins. I try to speak to those beside me, but we can't find our common tongue, so we cry. All of us making noise with no form. We are all from different and gone countries. I struggle beside their noise, birth is a tower, I now know. Eventually I'm picked up and gawked at by what must be my parents. It's not true, what they say – that you know them immediately. It's a myth, I think, that children feel bound to their blood, that when we look upon our mother for the first time, we see our home. Anywhere can be a home, so long as it feeds you.

Some things are indeed easier before language gets in the way. When you only have a few words, each one is a complete sentence, is a noun and a verb at once that carries the tremendous weight of the world. Point and say what you need and receive it: Water, Milk, Home, Mom, Food, Sleep, and eventually but not nearly so urgently, your own Name.

I admit to Christian eventually that when we met, I had been following him. He laughs and tells me of course he already knew. He remembered me from the store because my eye shadow was always so bright and messy and he was struck how a person could look so ugly and lovely all at the same time. And to think, I'd thought I blended. Even through your awful make-up, he says, I could tell you were pretty. He waits a beat, then finishes the sentence – pretty *gay*. I punch him lightly on the arm at this compliment deflected into its sweet jab. We're sitting in Prospect Park on a little bench tucked away out of the sun in the trees. From here, with our collective bad eyesight, the families playing on the far hill aren't so much individuals as mobs of colour, separate from each other but part of the same thick swirling mess, like a moving painting. I see how they're only worried about each other's joy, and not terrified by this unseasonably warm day in the middle of December. Do you want one, he asks? Assuming he means a child, I scoff and get all grand in my manner, say it's the end of the world and beautiful outside, and I'm just trying to make it as long as I can and it's probably the most selfish and irresponsible thing a person can do, worse than driving a car, worse than eating meat, I can't even look at some of these families now without getting a little sick. Then I look over to see that he was just offering me a cigarette.

The best way to learn yourself and a place is to walk. No music, no direction, no errands or objectives in mind, just follow the little compass in your chest and be drawn. Each time I walk this city, I find a different one there. Each time I walk, I'm different. It's not this city I want to be a part of, but everywhere at once, embedded deep in the design – nothing as grandiose as a keystone; more a human tooth buried somewhere unremarkable in the slow-dissolving architecture.

The internet is one big sensitive organ with untold nerve endings. You can even put your fingers inside it. At twelve, I discover an erotica website simply by typing 'porn + gay' which I type in as a joke, I tell myself, and there I learn what's possible in a story, how desire must have a structure and a shape. The stories are all coaches and their favourite players, or two boys stranded on a deserted island, or best friends snowed in at their family's cabin. The stories begin in media res with a protagonist longing for their object of desire and the stories end when the act is finished. Never a coda or even a concluding gesture. Never any fall-out or repercussions resulting from having acted, no speaker forced to reckon with the deep shame of what they've just made their body do. Most often they are written in the voice of someone like me, a child, a first encounter.

I message the authors, believing they're my age, just more accomplished, and far better writers. When they tell me what they want to do to my body, I learn what my body is capable of. They give me a language with which to imagine myself not dead inside. Later, in college, I learn that Althusser calls this interpellation, to be called a thing and then to either reject it or rise into that calling. None of these authors, I eventually learn, are my age, just old men wearing kids' faces. After a few weeks of messaging, the men reveal themselves as men, which I can later see buried in their syntax, the slang always landing just a bit off, from some bygone era. They use someone else's pictures, hiding behind a child's smile, maybe got the photos from someone like me, which gives me hope that there are others out there. That we're not all just fated to be old and hungry for what we've lost.

I never meet up with any of the men, but I do send pictures. The technology being clunkier then, I have to use a separate camera and auxiliary cable to upload them one at a time. Posing in front of my father's library, family portraits turned down in the background. Sitting cross-legged on the big brown leather chair. Every time I send a photo, these men lose their minds. They type their replies in all caps with bad punctuation, urgent and misspelled. They promise me anything I want. I've never felt so looked at in my life. I'll never be so looked at again.

At the Jewish socialist summer camp for monied kids from the tri-state area we sing Zog Nit Keynmol. We sing the Libertade. We work in the garden digging up weeds. We sleep in bunks. We eat lentils and bread. We are read to from the old books, and sing around a fire, eating s'mores, one each, though sometimes we sneak more. Here, in the Massachusetts woods, we replicate the Kibbutz, we all pitch in, all make songs. We march out into the woods and build fires and pretend to be regular boys. Here, among only Jews, we are suddenly good at sports, and we spike up our hair with copious amounts of gel, preparing to talk to girls. We imagine girls enjoy hair that is hard as plastic and shaped into a blade. We wear cargo shorts and stuff our pockets with dinner rolls. I stare too long in the changing room and, still, they accept me as one of their own. Here we are all outdoor boys until we break out into rashes that require steroidal creams. Here, we stay up at night and tell ghost stories about American ghosts. We sneak out of our bunks in hoodies, stealing into the cold summer nights to be wild in the trees. The only place I've ever been one of many. Until, one summer, my grandparents refuse to keep paying for it, insisting I learn the meaning of a dollar, which I find out quickly doesn't mean studying money so much as beginning to understand that we must sacrifice our time and labour for a small amount of it. So I stay home the next summer to work at the local pizza shop, and suddenly I am no longer one of the boys and never quite am one again. It ends as quick as that. I suppose in the end, every utopia is funded by this other lesser world, that to imagine a better world means at least you have to have the means to imagine it.

My last year in college, the theatre department puts on the classic play about a bunch of gay men in New York City. The play was first written in 1968 well before HIV/AIDS restructured the whole neighbourhood. In the play, they dance around and eat cake and are perfect bitches to each other. It's extra sad, because we all know what waits for them after the curtain falls. It's like watching from the other side of an apocalypse. The sadness of seeing a child do almost anything, knowing what waits for them when they eventually grow up. After the show, a group of us play the game the characters played, where you have to call the person you love most and tell them you love them. When it's my turn, of course, I call Edwin. He'd died earlier that semester and I haven't told anyone. I pretend to let it ring knowing full well the number's been disconnected. Had to stop calling it weeks ago. I left so many messages breathing – heavy wordless grunting, imagining him next to me – I hope his mother didn't listen. I pretend the answering machine's picked up, *It's the machine*, I say and wait a beat for the imaginary beep. *I love you, you know that, always have*, and everyone hoots and hollers as I press the red button to dead the call. And for a moment, in that room with all my living friends, he's alive again. And then it's the next person's turn to confess.

I read the news stories of farmers drinking pesticides to protest Monsanto destroying their livelihood by engineering plants with suicide seeds – seeds that die after each planting. I read about the fruit vendor Mohamed Bouazizi in Tunisia who inaugurated the Arab Spring. I read about the monks who lit themselves on fire to protest their government's violence. I listen to that Rage Against the Machine album with the burning monk on the cover.

What I don't manage to read is the news about the people who lit themselves on fire in Chicago. In East Texas. In Greece, or Israel, or Bulgaria, or Poland, or India, or China, or Saudi Arabia or —, or —, or —.

Mom's driving our boxy grey sedan back from the hospital. I've just got my booster shot for those three witches, tetanus, diphtheria, and pertussis. It didn't hurt, but I cried anyway, missing when I was younger and crying could get me anything I wanted. From the passenger side, Dad's humming a popular tune badly, something that might have once been a classic rock & roll standard if the band had laryngitis and aphasia and also decided to change the melody altogether. I'm in the backseat rolling my eyes at everything they say, as is my way of late. Mom carries a tiredness in her face, as if she's been up for months straight, calculating some impossible equation. As Dad hits the climax 'after we talked / I knew this was a dream . . .' she turns us swift into traffic, as if it's nothing, hands at ten and two on the wheel, and we're side-swiped by a group of kids, newly licensed, Jimmy Eat World blasting in their speakers. She's up against the window, jolted once, hard. Her head against the glass makes a clean sound you can almost hear over the bruising metal. No blood, a little jostled, something you'd hardly remember if not for all the yelling. Dad's furious as someone playing a father on television. The kids in the other car are crying hard, especially when they look at me, twelve but small for my age, looking more like a solid eight. Since the accident isn't so bad, he calms the children with one scolding finger, exchanges insurance information. We go back to the doctor to get me looked at. There are no signs of trauma or anything wrong. I giggle when the doctor makes a silly face. Everyone's relieved. Mom's tired; but, then, everything makes her tired these days – sorrow's been slow-feasting on her serotonin and her new meds haven't balanced out yet. She lies down on the couch with me in her arms, even though I'm too big for it. We sleep peacefully for a time in this man-made lake until I grow hungry and want to eat. I want fruit roll-ups and gushers. I want the sweet stuff other kids get to have for snacks. I cry like a little kid, but she isn't there. When no one comes to comfort me – when I realise there's no one left to cry for – I go make myself a peanut butter sandwich. Dad comes home from work just before the night comes on and it's only then we discover Mom's emptied her closet and the damaged sedan has vanished from the driveway. Even before she left, she was already gone.

Boxing up the small library at some newly dead man's apartment, I flip open his copy of an old Woolf novel to find handwriting on the inside cover. It's a small but loud thing. I've been working in this apartment for the past several hours, placing books into boxes, knowing this guy is in some way all around me . . . but something hits different now, seeing the ghost imprint of his hand there. The writing itself isn't remarkable, has nothing to do with the text – just a list of things to purchase: chicken, eggs, cabbage, flowers. And there he is, for a moment, alive again, ready to go about his life. To make one of countless unremarkable dinners.

In the comically tight basement bathroom of a gay bar in Bushwick, I catch my face in the mirror and hardly recognise who's staring back. I've just done a bump off a stranger's wrist following which he came on the floor like a dog. He mumbled a small thanks and left literal seconds after finishing, and now I'm here alone. Feeling emptier than I've ever felt . . . though that can't possibly be true. Hyperbole is a way of being in the world that's always suited me – drama, my favourite cousin. Some popular song is distorting into unfamiliar patchworks of sound through the floorboards and people waiting in line for the toilet are trying to make themselves heard over it. When I go to rinse my mouth out, I'm confronted with myself, unnaturally red in the filtered light, surprised by who's looking back. Not not me but also, not me. Replicant. Pod girl. Nothing person. Hunger making me ugly. The skin's sitting all strange on the cheekbones, a mask contorted with gone pleasure. Sweatier than I'd thought, more manic behind the eyes, like there's an animal trapped inside. So I do what I can to control it, make the face smile, lift the eyebrows up to appear inviting, then lower them back down to unlock the door.

Some idiot kids spray-paint swastikas in the cemetery behind our synagogue and the whole town gets together to march against hate. Hate is the vaguest concept I can imagine; it means even less than love. Everyone's dressed up for the occasion, and I couldn't feel farther away. I'm 75 per cent sure I know the kids who did it, using spray cans from the local hardware store and then throwing them away in the appropriately labelled recycling bins, and I'm almost a hundred per cent sure they aren't actually Antisemites or anything. They just wanted to make something happen. Sometimes life in this suburb grows so stagnant that to make anything move is an accomplishment. Time soldiers forward, predicable and slow as a bone healing wrong, and sometimes all you want to do is light a fire to see what burns or breaks. After the march, speaker after speaker takes to the podium on the steps of the public library, each of them like well-manicured hedges. Each of them ready, with urgency flashing in their eyes, to guide the way forward so that we as a community can *overcome hate*. You can see in their straightened postures the purpose this gives them and it makes me sick. Knowing I have classmates who can't afford even the gross school lunches, seeing the bombs on television falling on Baghdad like some kind of pageant, and this was my neighbours' cause – their great stand – standing up against the drawings of children? I almost wish it was me who defaced the gravestones. In fact, I'm almost tempted to stand up right now and confess. After this, I start drawing them over and over in my notebook, those brutal unfinished windows, little inherited boxes of death, wanting to make anything happen, filling up whole pages then tearing them into illegible shreds, throwing the confetti in the air, then starting over again.

A man sets up his telescope at an abandoned intersection just outside my college town and lets whoever comes by look through it. It's a good telescope, almost professional. He's not affiliated with the university but lives here and loves the stars, so every week he sets up his device and if you know someone who's been, or know someone who knows someone, or just happen to be walking by, you can take a gander. Tonight, through the slim aperture, if I position my eye just right, I can see the craggy surface of the Martian planet. Desert planet. Our own burnt orange future. He tells us the popular theory, that Mars was once just like us but then something catastrophic happened, and all life was burnt clean off its surface. I keep seeing the reports – a hundred years, fifty years, just three years left – to reverse, to revise, to change, to devise, to have a revolution of our most basic means of thought, an unprecedented paradigm shift. Solar panels, carbon capture, and on and on. *We're losing*, I keep thinking, as people insist science will save us. The *we* is everything that breathes. I look to who controls the bodies that control the science, what interest is it to survive and who stands to profit off all this survival? In the movies, the world's governments always come together to stop the meteorite, but in real life politicians say *existential dread* and keep making backroom deals to steady the price of corn and oil. It's beautiful, the planet bobbing up there like a dead red apple floating in a big black lake. Feels as if I'm peering through time into our future, the telescope looking through a mirror straight through time. A future that isn't a future at all, that defies the very mind who thinks it, its linear inevitability, our own personhood obliterated within the precision of that convex glass lens. The cosmos start to spin around me, as they always do when I sense our true place in them, planets and galaxies cut through with telephone wires, and I find myself spinning with it, collapsing, knocking over the telescope only to wake up what feels like a century later to a shadowy figure hovering over me saying, *you're fine, kid – you're gonna to be just fine*.

The package arrives that next week inside a manila envelope with three stamps. The stamps have Israeli flags on them, good for life, bought and paid for. *Gross*, I think. There is an old-timey wax seal on the envelope with a symbol that looks vaguely like a goat. Inside the envelope: a small sample of water in the kind of soft plastic packets you'd get free lube in at a bar or clinic.

I text Dad, *got your god lube . . .* He replies, *Ezra meyn ingel, meyn boychik, use it in your hair, it will never fall out. Then perhaps, you can post about it.* I go immediately to examine my hairline in the mirror. Asshole. Still looks alright, although maybe receded a half centimetre, depending on the angle of the light? Shit, there goes beauty.

I forget for a week until I notice the packet lying there in the ceramic dish where I put my mail and key. I tear it open between my teeth and use it to water my saddest succulent, a red aeonium I've named Julianne Moore that looks like one giant wet eye. Julianne Moore neither grows faster nor dies on the spot. She just goes on being a succulent, performing her own tiny miracles – transforming light into food, breathing carbon, living on despite having no good reason.

Passovers we make the drive to Mom's mom's apartment on the Upper West Side. The Haggadah here is more activist than religious and the ritual often includes singing black spirituals and civil rights era protest songs without nuance or analysis. A bunch of white people sitting around a table fat with unleavened Chinese takeout, singing about breaking the bonds of slavery. The seder plate is one of the few things we make ourselves. The songs I learned at camp come in handy here, the stories we tell and retell as if they were our own.

The apartment's got one room big enough for all nine of us around the long oak table. The walls are covered in prints by Soviet agitprop artists, smiling red faces eating corn and holding sickles, while a pop-art-inspired painting of Marx looms down fatherly over the table, oddly comfortable in his bourgeois gold frame. My grandparents are there, my dad and me, Great Uncle Charlie and Great Aunt Ruth and their adult children, who even to a more or less formal affair wear band t-shirts and ripped jeans, which Dad tells me they can do only because they're rich. They all grew distant after Mom disappeared (too much sadness to face – first her brother dying, then her taking off how she did) but if anyone ever thought to say so directly, they would deny and get defensive, so it never comes up. This is the once a year we see them.

I'm the only one who brings a dish, meringue cookies with chocolate chips. As always, we wash each other's hands from the same bowl, which seems less hygienic than doing nothing at all. Before we can eat, Grandpa launches into the story of his father, Herschel. The story is always a little different, but always goes a little like this:

> In Russia, early in the revolution, Herschel organised the workers at the factory. So beloved was Herschel, there's a monument of his likeness in their town. A bronze statue by the river docks of the man himself, holding a bar of soap like a rock in his hand. It's legend there how he stood up to the factory owner and led the labourers with torches to the row of mansions and burned down a piece of their fortunes from the inside. He had to flee for America before retribution could come, leaving his wife and daughter behind – seeds germinating back in the old country. We all are here because of that sacrifice, and must lament having never met such a great man as Herschel.

If he were really brave, he would have stayed, I think every time Grandpa tells it. And none of this would have had to follow.

My last summer, everyone's playing Pokémon Go. You see people walking around in groups with faces bowed into their phones, which isn't new, but now they're using them to look at the world. The designers have made it so every part of the city is filled with these invisible monsters. An augmented reality mobile game it's called, and it does just that, populates the city with digital creatures. Below this bench in Union Square, there's a Raticate. Sitting beside you on the J Train might be a Slowpoke looking forlornly out the window. At the top of the Empire State Building, a Pidgey is posing next to your family, grinning in the way only a cartoon bird-monster can. Groups of friends walk in packs, staring through their screens trying to find rare Pokémon hiding amongst us in the city, invisible to the naked eye. *Corny ass street gangs*, mumbles an old woman beside me in the park. The game can be a metaphor for anything really – any occluded illness, subculture, history – anything that might be hidden just out of sight.

Not wanting to be left entirely out of the discourse, I purchase the game and open it lying naked on my bed beneath the alchemical drone of my ceiling fan. Following the brief tutorial, where I design my avatar to look vaguely like me, only butcher, and then name him Gwendolyn, the game boots up and I open the viewfinder to look around. I'm horrified by what appears on my screen. My room is filled with them. Literally dozens, gathered around me, none looking like any Pokémon I've ever seen but more like regular people, wearing all manner of strange garments, just staring at me. I turn around three-hundred-sixty degrees watching them watching me. In gowns, and wigs, and girdles, and rags, and robes. None of them move; they just stare unblinking, eyes following the camera's lens. My breathing is shallow as a grave dug with a spoon and I look back and forth, frantic, between the phone screen and the room. Closest to me is a small boy caked in soot, a child who appears to have known unspeakable labour, his eyes are cartoon-big, he might be my cousin. I reach out to thumb the dirt from his cheek, only to see, on the screen, my hand pass clean through his pitiful face, and he leaps back clutching at his head as if I've wounded him. I pull back hard too, somehow hurt by my own unintended violence. Fuck this. I grip the phone and slow-panic swipe up, holding down my thumb to delete the game forever.

I'm never able to shake the feeling that they're in here with me – I move through the apartment slowly now, undress beneath a towel, ask if they approve of my outfits, start making jokes to my empty room and pretend I can hear them laughing back.

It's no accident I join the 27 Club, although a bit embarrassing to admit I join it on purpose. Of the group of them – Basquiat, Winehouse, Morrison, Cobain, Hendrix, Joplin – I like Morrison the least, which means we likely have the most in common. Not the womanising, alcoholism, or snakeskin pants. But maybe it's the presumptive way of moving through the world, the bad poetry, the wild hair. I wonder how many suicides, artists especially, plot their leaving around this number. Younger than Christ, older than Rimbaud when he stopped writing. Lucky for me I never made any music publicly, never tried to leave my 'mark' on the world, really – how embarrassing would that be? Art is so embarrassing, and if it isn't at first blush, just give it a few years, it will be. Someone might make the accusation this is just a publicity stunt, and they wouldn't be wrong, though would be hard-pressed to say exactly for what. Survivability? Living grief? Giving up my own two lungs with the hope it'll give someone a little more good air to breathe?

When we couldn't find any weed, when the liquor cabinets ran dry and no one had their fake ID, after sucking off our parents' elaborate medicine cabinets, too tired to venture down to D-Block for more pills, all it would take was a little bit of gasoline and a rag. You could find it just about anywhere. You huffed it in, and then it felt like you were flying through a chemical sponge. You'd feel the slightest nausea, but then there's a twitching light timed in perfect sequence with whatever music is on. Like a lighthouse in the skull, just like a lighthouse. That's how it went, a little bit of gasoline on a rag and then you breathed the entire rag in, feeling it pulse right through your nervous system. The nervous system either works with you, or against. How do you say it? Strangely worded. Wounded, like. I liked it. First time, we were in the unfinished basement off the garage at Edwin's mom's house where she kept the gas canister for their generator. He doused the rag's middle then held it up to my mouth and said *breathe*. I breathed. His other hand pressed against the back of my neck. The feeling swallowed me. I didn't pass out or anything but did go limp and let him do whatever he wanted. I pretended it was the drug that opened me like that but of course it was only an opening for my own (un)doing, only a mask I could become my true and thirsty self inside.

Mom comes back to the apartment only a handful of times and each visit she's less and less there. I assume it's out of some inherited sense of obligation, *this is what a mother does*, pulls her body back here to sit at our metal kitchen table and fumble around gawking at the cage of her former life. Each time, there are fewer signs of her in the home until you wouldn't be able to tell she ever lived here at all. She even disappears from the picture frames as the photographs are slowly replaced. There's always a new hairdo and a purpose, to collect her fur coat or to sign some paperwork, and each time she acts like everything's fine – tells me stories about her life. There's a new man in Taos with whom she's starting an art gallery in her asymmetrical bob. She's heading off for a year to WOOF on an organic plum farm in northern Oregon in feathered bangs. She's settling down with a couple in Detroit and they're renovating an old house – she shows me pictures of the house and the couple with her head shaved close. The visits come further and farther apart until they stop all together, as do the calls, until we all finally give up the scripts we've inherited and accept instead the life we have in front of us.

My last year is the last year for many rodents with beautiful names:

Bettongia anhydra, Conilurus capricornensis, Dusicyon avus, Leporillus apicalis, Melomys rubicola, Notomys robustus, Pennatomys nivalis, Pipistrellus murrayi, Pseudomys auratus.

And many many birds as well:

Acrocephalus luscinius, Acrocephalus musae, Acrocephalus nijoi, Acrocephalus yamashinae, Aegolius gradyi, Akialoa ellisiana, Akialoa lanaiensis, Akialoa stejnegeri, Alectro-enas payandeei, Aplonis ulietensis, Bermuteo avivorus, Chenonetta finschi, Coenocorypha barrierensis, Coeno-corypha iredalei, Colaptes oceanicus, Columba thiriouxi, Dryolimnas augusti, Eclectus infectus, Foudia delloni, Hemi-gnathus lucidus, Himatione fraithii, Loxops wolstenholmei, Nesoenas cicur, Nyctanassa carcinocatactes, Pipilo naufragus, Porphyrio paepae, Prosobonia cancellata, Pyrocephalus dubius, Tachybaptus rufolavatus, Tribonyx hodgenorum, Zosterops conspicillatus, Zosterops semiflavus.

Don't get me started on all the bugs.
Our names almost sound like spells as they leave us.

In one version of my death, I'm lifted from the hospital bed and carried away by this vast and humming river of birds, rats, and insects. All of us never to be heard from again.

This happened in a small town outside of what is now Minsk. There was a boy who moved to study at yeshiva and spent all his days reading. All his days the boy was in deep conversation with dead scholars; all his days, he transcribed only what had previously been said. Word for word, their language moved through his hand. He surrounded himself with the words of only the holiest men. He was, after all, apprenticing himself to holiness. Every day, between his dormitory and the school, he'd pass a boy around his age begging for food. The boy was just like him, aside from being bedraggled and gallowed by hunger that left him with no time for the study of language. Every day, the learned boy passed by the other offering the occasional crust of bread. This story doesn't end how you'd like it to. The begging boy wasn't god, waiting to impart a critical lesson, or to allocate a station. No. One day on his way to school, the begging boy took a knife and slit the learned boy's throat from ear to ear, escaping with what little money he had and his satchel of food. The dead boy's papers caught the wind and were carried off into the rivers and waved there in the branches like new leaves. Holier than scripture, this lesson tells of what any lord will not do when some have not.

ERICKA: you good?

EZRA: Good good.

EZRA: Good enough.

EZRA: Been gooder but also been less good.

EZRA: Good grief. Good riddance, Yaknow? Hby?

ERICKA: #same

I make a city with my hands. I place angels in the city and people the buildings with televisions.

Love is just another thing that happens to you, like a rash or a bad radish or a car accident. My life makes more sense once I realise this simple, irrefutable fact. I meet Arnold at the tail end of college. We've followed each other on Tumblr for a few years, having similar interests in the occult and '90s fashion, but never realised we live in the same town until he posted a picture of a patty melt from an iconic local dinner. Ten years my senior, Arnold stuck around after his own graduation to build his life. Not exactly a *failure to launch* situation, since he has a real job and does community work here. He lives in the bottom floor of this old blue Victorian on the edge of town. I'm an English major with nothing else to do, so when I mention on our third date at the one semi-gay bar in town that I have to move out of the dorms at the end of the month, he suggests I move into the ol' blue house. When the month ends, I go ahead and do just that.

It's an interesting way to get to know someone, seeing their life from the inside out. Strips away any pretence or per-formance. Before the first night ends, you'll both have to shit and put in your mouthguard and apply your various elaborate night-creams. He's quick and discreet about it, locking the door, playing music on his phone while I do my business with it half open, still used to communal dorm bathrooms.

Arnold is bald with a little moustache, like the Monopoly man but swoll. He seems like a good man, emphasis on man, meaning a proper adult. He wears starched striped shirts with buttons he buttons up all the way to his razor-burned neck before driving his silver Impreza to work at the youth services non-profit. He owns his property, has dinner parties, and a 401(k). The night I move in is the first proper night I've spent with him; before this we'd just fooled around in his car like a couple kids. He unbuttons his shirt and folds it into a crisp retail display before placing it in his dry-cleaning bag. *What a psychopath*, I think. When we have sex, I can tell he thinks he's making love to me; it's almost entirely eye contact, as if eye contact could be a kind of penetration – which clearly, it can, but this was not. I accept him inside me, legs open wide – how you'd hug a drunk uncle – below the beige Pottery Barn curtains blowing in a night-gust of wind to reveal a full and exaggerated swollen moon. I swallow a laugh: how is this my life?

Life here is simple and meticulously curated. Like living in a private museum or being a long-term guest in the house of a friend's wealthy parent. There are various replica indigenous masks on the walls from Arnold's extensive travels. There is a cabinet whose entire purpose is to display small glass figurines, like a grandmother or that Tennessee Williams play I haven't seen but know is canonical, gay, and decidedly sad. I have the bottom two drawers of a dresser for my things and that's it, which is fine, never having been much one for things, or at least never having had much of a chance to accumulate them.

We have a nice little life, Arnold and me. I grow easily into my domestic duties. I already cook okay and now learn how to clean properly. He likes when I wear a little apron and nothing else. It's a fun bit until he grows to expect it – laying out the black apron on the kitchen island when it's time – then it becomes a kind of labour, and I just go ahead and consider that rent.

Alone in the house most of the day while Arnold's at work, I spend hours arranging and rearranging everything just so. Most of my friends have moved on to jobs in cities or at least better towns, but the few who remain come over every now and then to drink on our porch while Arnold reads inside.

Slowly, though, even they stop coming by, unable to really vibe with this new grown-af lifestyle. They want to do dumb kid shit, turn up and make bad decisions – the kind I understand and occasionally even yearn for.

Dad's been too busy fundraising for the new synagogue to come visit, so I send him pictures of our little life here. I don't want the pictures to look too staged, but want the home to appear lived in, so I dishevel the slipcover, unpin the curtains, rearrange some plants. *Nice flowers*, he replies to the photograph of the bay window overlooking the neighbour's garden, which I never said was ours but don't correct him either.

Sundays we splay out on the chaise, listening to records and flailing around like goofballs. Sometimes, I do an interpretive dance to some old soul record and he'll laugh, recording it on his phone. Other times, he'll put on an opera I know nothing about, and we'll sit quietly on the couch listening through its movements. At least once a record's turn, the contralto or mezzo-soprano will be singing some exaggerated grief and it will rise up overtaking him and he'll begin sobbing and shaking there on the couch. I do my best to make up the stories in my head, but even when I come up empty, all that energy is enough to make me start crying alongside him, how the right resonant note can shatter a glass across the room. And I find myself crying, not at the opera, but at the man beside me, letting all that opera pass through his large and trembling frame like a train carrying animals through the night.

Angels in the city and people the buildings—

I meet his half-sister Constance, a few months in when she comes to visit from Hartford and the whole meal she refuses to look at me, like I'm some kind of boy-ghost that might go away if simply ignored. We all sit at the table together, and they spend the dinner talking about people I've never heard of: family members or famous activists or dead philosophers. I don't recognise any of the names. Arnold has spatchcocked and roasted a chicken with some turnips. I do my best to smile when they both do and politely cut into my bird. I ask her to pass the gravy, but maybe I ask it too softly, so I just quietly eat my dry and undressed meat. I'm supposed to be 'the room-mate', he tells me moments before she arrives without offering any explanation as to why.

After we've finished the meal, she turns her attention to me for the first time. *What's up with you*, she asks, *do you speak?* Admittedly not the most welcoming address, and suddenly it's as if I'm standing before a judge someplace I don't speak the language.

Uhh. Nothing. I mean, yes I do. I'm reading a book about mushrooms actually and, um, looking for a job.

A silence follows us here and sits on the table like another split bird. *Alright Arnold*, she says rolling her eyes at the whole house, *you keep doing you*. I'm not quite sure how to take this, but can tell I've done something wrong. Later that night, I think to ask after he's cum inside me, but by the time I get up the courage to speak, he's already asleep.

Against Arnold's wishes, I get a job to fill my time. The only work I can find that will hire someone with my lack of experience, interest, and drive is as an evening security guard for a warehouse. It's a twenty-minute bike ride away, down in an empty, unlit part of town filled with self-storage units and commercial lots. It's a climate-controlled building rented out to private businesses where they store many things: flowers, seed and farm equipment, refrigerated meats. In some rooms, there are buckets and buckets of larkspur, scabiosa, roses, and zinnias; in other rooms, there are carcasses hanging from hooks wrapped in plastic.

The shift stretches through the night and ends near dawn, and between my rounds I sit at a desk, drinking burnt coffee. I add the occasional splash of whiskey like I've seen them do in the movies.

The secret delight of my job is I'm basically being paid to read. I glance up every now and then at the monitors, but mostly what I do is revisit the books I've already forgotten from high school. *Giovanni's Room*, *Mrs Dalloway*, any Salinger. Since nothing ever happens here besides the occasional teens pulling into our parking lot to smoke weed, I dive into books where the ordinary is made to seem epic. Books that help me remember to enhance the minutiae of the common minute. Where I can figure myself as the protagonist of my own small story, poking my head into meat lockers, shining my flashlight onto silent rooms stacked high with electronics. Books where, even if all you're doing is guarding some flowers, someone's gotta end up dead.

Every so often, Arnold has friends over and we play a board game. He either cooks or we order in pizza or fried chicken. Mostly we play one of those multi-hour-long colonising games where you have to settle something, or defend a territory, or build a railroad. I like having other voices in the house. Once in a while, after the carafe of wine's emptied and someone's managed to conquer the small flat world, Arnold will put on a record and we'll play around together. I've never done anything like this before, but it seems just like the normal thing grown folks do. The first time I'm a bit unsure, I don't know how best to use my body or have my body be made use of, but then I grow to love it – becoming multiple like that, all those limbs, like we're a single insect writhing there on the grey rug. Other times, I'm a bridge between two men, a wet filament lighting up the space between them. They're always Arnold's age or a little older, and it feels like I'm being welcomed into something, a secret club or maybe this is adulthood. He met most of them on hookup apps years ago and now they've just become regular friends. Some nights, they stay over; other nights, they leave right after we're done. It's nice when it's the same friends, a little taste of community, familiar voices in the house. Sometimes we'll play a game without a story.

I like those best, where you rearrange letters into a common language, or have to recall the names of long-dead movie stars or the end date of some terrible war.

I give this city a name, I name this city after angels.

Tonight gets ugly because I'm not up for anything following Catan. Arnold's never acted quite like this before, but he's legit mad. Noam is a small Jewish guy, mid-forties, slight build but nice eyes. He's whatever. He's just moved to town after some kind of heartbreak and Arnold wanted to show him a good time. I mean he's fine – I've for sure had worse – but I just wasn't in the mood for anything, and this is all getting a bit predictable. We're on like the eighth Thursday in a row that's supposed to go from board game and wine to that old Eartha Kitt record and a threesome, and honestly, it's getting kind of boring.

After winning the game, Noam is feeling really big on himself, chest puffed up, little fish hooked up onto the deck of a ship. He's gloating and wine-glowing and somehow from the other end of the couch manages to spring up leaping at me and starts going at my neck like he's still collecting wheat. It feels like being covered by a living blanket. After letting him go on a bit, I make a yucked-out guttural noise and push him off, straighten my shirt and go to the bathroom to catch my breath.

My face floats there in the mirror – suddenly unmoored from my body, and I can just make out the little kid I was in photographs. When I get back to the living room, it's eerie quiet beneath the music and Noam is putting on his dark blue suit jacket to leave. He says something hot under his breath to Arnold and shakes his head. The door closes behind him, the record nears its end – *I am without my love*, Eartha sings, (*without my love*) – and Arnold flies off into an ugly electricity.

He can't believe I'd embarrass him and his friend like that. Noam's been having a really hard time making friends since moving to town, he says, and he expected me to be a little more welcoming. It's not like he's asking much of me. I tell him I hate feeling sorry for people, it's so not hot, and this guy reeked of sorry. So sorry (not sorry), and I roll my eyes like a child.

This is new for us; usually when he gets even a little mad, I get bone quiet. My saying anything at all means something, but it takes a moment before we can name what that something is. In that pause, before naming it, he almost doubles in size and throws what's left of the porterhouse on its serving platter across the room. We're silent while the record finishes, dissolving into metered felt clicks, the dish on the ground slowly leaks gravy onto the grey Pottery Barn rug. We stand there in that pulsing silence until I start to feel the rug fibres taking on fat and so, in a gesture of supplication, I move to clean up the gravy.

He flips the record and her voice begins anew – *i wanna go to the devil*. He asks if I want a ride to the warehouse, like nothing happened. *I'm good*, I say; *I love you*, I say, and even the blue pilot lights on the stove know I'm lying. Moments later, I'm piloting my bike out onto the shoulder of the highway, the asphalt wet and bright below me, riding forward toward some kind of security.

Before Arnold, I thought that heartbreak was the worst thing that can happen to you. I've had my fair share. Am familiar enough with the deep pit of it, in fact have learned to love it, to make a home down there.

Historically, love is considered a sign of lunacy. Scientists say it lights up the same section of the brain that responds to addiction, opioids, and the moon. Arnold's always seemed gentle enough. Sure, he gets mad, but everyone gets a little mad sometimes, and he's manageable. Until, of course, he isn't.

I've been drinking since getting off my shift at the warehouse, strolling through the nearby towns, unsure how my life has become this life and so I've decided to drink about it. Hash out some things in the old way, inside my own dull-grey haze. A mouth-shaped bruise has appeared on my neck from Noam and I'm annoyed I'll have to look at it for another week. That people will make jokes and I'll have to laugh. I kill a bottle of something cheap and clear and then another of something dark.

When I finally come home, Arnold's sitting upright in the leather recliner in the morning's half-light, waiting up like a street between skyscrapers. His face looks strange, pasted onto someone else's face. He's quiet in an empty kind of way. I lean in for a kiss and I'm kissing a rubber mask. I'm about to speak when I hear him whisper, *You don't get to do that*. He rises and I don't know exactly what he means, but I'm tired and just want to lie down. *What don't I get to do?*

It's only when he grips my neck that I realise how much bigger he is than me, and he lifts me up how a mother lion disciplines her cub, dragging me all the way to the hall closet with the umbrellas and raincoats. I'm wasted enough that I don't resist being moved, though the pressure on my neck feels almost dangerous. A part of me likes being held, even under these circumstances, a point of stability in this dizzying world. He lowers me into the closet like I'm an extension cord and I hear the lock click home.

I laugh for a bit at the metaphor swimming around in my head – after all these years, wasted in the closet again. I throw up into his rainboots. Some minor justice. For a moment, relief floods through me – at last, I don't have to *do* or *be* anything, don't even have to stand up to brush my teeth, and isn't this the obvious conclusion of all my indecision? That, by following the path of least resistance, I end up here on the ground, in perfect darkness, wearing the bottom of an expensive wool peacoat for a hat. It is something adjacent to relief. That is, until I sober up.

In the ER, I make a city with my hands. I place angels in the city and people the buildings with televisions. I dream who lives on what blocks and imagine how the community thrums, all the sounds of the marketplaces, subways, and penny arcades. I give this city a name, I name this city after angels, this city I make with my hands.

Here in the hospital, for four days and four nights, I do what I can to not think about my circumstance. Dehydration, the doctors say. The nurses take care of me, treat me like a child again, which is the thing I love most about illness.

Two days, I spent in Arnold's closet until finally managing to pull myself through the tiny window out into the yard, where someone called the cops, following which I was brought here. I can't imagine what I must have looked like, crawling all dybbuk-like across the neighbours' immaculately manicured lawns, lol.

I'm hooked up to so many tubes I might as well be a tractor ploughing a dead planet in some science-fiction novel. I've likely already lost my job at the warehouse. My phone's been long dead and in this small-town hospital there are no televisions, so I have to invent this little world for me to play in. The brain does that, makes up little games to avoid itself.

At first, the police are my only visitors. They want to know what happened, who did this, was something even done; they want Arnold's name. I don't say a thing of course. If I know anything at all, it's that I fucking hate cops. Anyways, I think it'll taste like rags in my mouth if I say his name out loud. It's not until my father comes to check on me – my expired college insurance must have called – that I actually speak, although given how bruised my trachea is, the sound comes out as a low hissing radiator. He prays over me, and for the first time I don't hate the sound of prayer, the Mi Sheberach at last becoming almost known to me. I mimic the sounds, and all our gone people are in this room with us now, even those we didn't know were ours. For the first time, I can feel what the words mean as they drag themselves out of me, not in terms of sense exactly, but sentiment. These prayers were sung well before any living person or civilisation and will outlive all of our mechanical noise. In this quiet way, in time and across it, we pray together.

My father's biggest fear is being in a small room slowly filling with water. He tells me this as though for the first time, whenever it comes up, which is surprisingly often, after I move back in with him following my stay at the hospital. His friends stay away while I'm recovering and all we do is watch movies. Movies it seems are the only common language we still share. Seven out of ten action films feature this scenario at some point. A small room in a valley is flooded by a city government's greed. Lovers are trapped in the compartment of a damaged Russian submarine. A cruise ship takes on water. Climate change relocates a vacation resort to the bottom of the ocean. A booby trap triggers, and some ancient king's tomb fills with the sea. And he'll turn to me, saying it just like this, *You know, Ezra, that's my biggest fear*, then turns back to the television, calm as a glass figurine, to keep watching as if he hadn't just seen his deepest nightmares come to life on screen, and I'll say, *I know, Dad*.

Water's never scared me, for some reason. Even that one time I was swimming and nearly got dragged off into the Long Island Sound by a rogue undertow. Small spaces either; they just tend to make me feel like I'm being held. Heights are fine as well. It might sound like a cop-out, but I really don't fear anything so much as my own mind, and the not-so-subtle way it can distort and disassemble any room. What I fear as well, I guess, is other people – awkward conversation, being seen and witnessed, being discussed, the standard metrics and methods of various social deaths. And what I truly fear *most*, if anyone were to ask, which my father never does, is not just that I've wasted this one precious life, but that I'll have to bear witness to other people appraising it, those who might have done so much more with this little platform of a body I've been gifted only to throw away, again and again, into the Hudson. These fears are less common in action movies, so Dad and I keep watching buildings explode and burn while I heal.

This happened in a town called Shoflet. The town lay just south of a lake where every day the people would make the several-mile-long pilgrimage to water, lower their heads to drink and then struggle back with filled buckets. The water was still clear then — god had not yet seen what humans were capable of. The villagers lived where they lived and loved their neighbours. They would share the food they grew, share the animals they butchered, and all was well. Only one day, when it was hot as tehom and the knife used to slice the goat's throat had not been properly blessed, and the animal cried out in such excruciating pain when it died, that the blood of everyone in the surrounding towns began to curdle inside them. There was a meeting to determine what was to be done to the butcher, to the rabbi who slept through his blessing, to the knife itself; and all the while, the goat meat rotted out in the field, so slowly did the bureaucracy of law move. Eventually they buried the knife, desanctified the rabbi, and fined the butcher. Even so, where the goat died a darkness spread over the land, and all the grasses turned bleach-white, its sacrifice for naught. The blood fed back into the soil and made the soil die. Death soon spread to the sea and the families invented a system of money by which to trade their goods. God so wept when he saw this, he cursed the water to salt. When the villagers came back to drink, their throats pickled, their children learned to float.

By chance, I happen upon my first May Day protest an hour and change from campus. We don't make it into the city often, aside from going to a concert or to buy hard-to-find drugs. Today, though, we're going to see our theatre professor in his debut one-person production of *Equus*, where he somehow plays Martin Dysart, Alan Strang, and the horse which will likely prove to be, to say the very least, memorable. But on our way to the play, we come upon a crowd filled with young people chanting behind black balaclavas, while a man stands on trashcans nearby, orating in Spanish. Floating in playful revolt above the boulevard are giant puppets that seem to be made only of cloth and sticks, in the shapes of various gods, monsters, and politicians. And I realise this may be more my kind of theatre.

Stepping into the crowd, we are carried along for a time like forever chemicals in a river. My friends are with me one minute and then suddenly my friends are dispersed – maybe off to the play? – and now all these new people become my friends. My ensemble. My company. I walk behind banners I can't read, though I admire their brilliant peacock colours. On all sides are kids in masks breaking the windows of the Wells Fargo, the Foot Locker, the Starbucks. They all have no pasts but the ones they've dragged here. I'm embarrassed by the fancy outfit I've put together for the theatre, the blazer with the gold octopus brooch, the tapered khakis, and my messy attempt at a smoky eye. I envy them, all of them. How they can make themselves a family not simply by how they dress, like a fraternity or the police, but by how they are protecting something at once more common and sacred than a bank or a sneaker store.

This distinction becomes even clearer when the police arrive and shoot off tear gas seemingly indiscriminately into the crowd – there are kids in strollers, an old man and his walker with a miniature megaphone hanging around his neck. The gas moves around us like new weather. Alone together and breathing in poison, all my language won't be enough – only substitutions will do. My eyes are two sick onions. My eyes are goats slaughtered wrong. My eyes, twin libraries burning.

May Day is, of course, also what the pilot says when the plane starts going down. A street medic finds me vomiting yellowish heat across the sidewalk. Wearing a red cross and a green mohawk, she stands over me and pours milk into the twin burning saucers of my eyes. In this way, I am welcomed, for a moment, into my new family.

Mom takes me to the river to feed the ducks. I'm wearing an outfit I'll cycle into hating then loving then hating again, depending when it happens to be in vogue. The height of a particular kind of early '90s fashion: neon graphic *Jurassic Park* t-shirt, black short-shorts, and some light-up sneakers. Lucky for me, this style comes back just in time for me to get my first Instagram account and I post the photo of Mom and me, looking like a faded advertisement, there on the hood of our wrangler, to moderate approval and comment.

We do this every month or so, collecting the heels of bread that have gone stale in one plastic sleeve and then carrying them down here to the river, a short drive from our apartment. Ten minutes in the car when you are child can feel like a life-time, and although we're just beneath the highway, it somehow feels as if we're deep in a proper wilderness. The river itself is man-made, an endless cement basin that carries water from the reservoir out to the treatment plant. Even so, the natural world floods in. There are ducks and turtles in the river; tadpoles and minnows and aquatic plants. There are men fishing on its banks who pull out the occasional small perch. Mom's in her high-waisted mom jeans and laughs when the wind blows her black wide-brimmed hat off as we chase it into the thinning pines.

What I don't realise at the time is that her brother has just died. Took his own life, no one says. What they do say is he chose the bottle over a house or a job or a woman. His body was found in his car just a few blocks from our apartment. Must have driven up from Queens to the suburbs. He'd been missing for a few weeks. Now Mom has to drive by the corner where they found him every day. Every day she has to drive past her brother. She unfurls the plastic sleeve and hands a piece of bread to me which I promptly eat and we both laugh. Her little duckling, she calls me, and I quack and I quack.

My synagogue signs me up for a free trip, so I go. *It's free*, Dad says, *you'd be stupid not to*, and in high school, I don't know enough to argue this faulty logic. That everything, in the end, has its price.

We're gathered in a swarm at JFK and a man with a goatee and messy top bun hands us gift bags which include, among other things, one hacky sack stitched with the Israeli flag. They tell us we're going home and forty fifteen-year-olds all nod along. They tell us to sing the national anthem so we make our way through the Hatikvah transliterated off printed sheets. Some of us tear up at the melody but don't know what it means. All of us are acne-drenched in cargo shorts, visors, and Birkenstocks. Most of us are from New York, or New Jersey, or Philadelphia – and then there's Aarom, a quiet kid from rural Wisconsin, the only Jew in his town. Aarom, sitting next to me on the flight, is so small my outstretched hand could just about cover the whole width of his pale back. He's scared to fly, I can tell, and our knees press against each other on and off the entire flight, and with each touch a current runs between us. I make sure to sit next to Aarom every chance I get.

As soon as we spill out of our plane into Ben Gurion Airport, we find ourselves standing around in small groups hacking our little Israeli flags. I have bad eye–foot coordination, apparently, and struggle to keep the flag in the air. The trip is oddly well co-ordinated with a precisely managed itinerary that doesn't seem to fit our scruffy pothead counsellors. We go to Tel Aviv; we ride the cable car to the top of Masada; we sleep in a Bedouin tent in the Negev and drink Coca-Cola; we plant trees in pre-dug holes that will be emptied for the next group of tourists; we go to the Wailing Wall separated by gender and take pictures there; we write down little prayers on paper and slip them into the holes (I ask for a boyfriend in precise detail, his demeanour and shape and length of hair, before tagging on an end to world hunger for good measure); we walk through the old city and haggle with vendors over weed pipes. All the other kids want to bring their future kids, they say, most likely together, so they too can share this one-of-a-kind experience. We sing songs and eat falafel and shakshuka, which we're told are Israeli foods.

Aarom and I bunk together, and some nights he lets me sleep in his bed so I can cuddle up next to him when it gets cold, which it does often in the desert. I don't *really* understand why we're here. Sure, it's a beautiful country, I think, looking out over someone else's desert – can someone even own a desert and, if so, how could it possibly be us? – so different from the astringent skyscrapers and fried drive-through windows I come from. It's clear, being here, that neither here nor back home, with its strip-malls and what the strip-malls cover up, is my home. If anything, my home is the endless empty parking lot fields growing crops of trash and plastic tumbleweed. My home is where my body breathes and nowhere else, where it's going and where it's been. Can someone just say a thing is theirs and it becomes so? Can you really go back to the neighbourhood your great-great-great-grandparents might have lived in and say, *This is my house?* Not caring who lives there? Years later, Aarom will return to this beautiful country and say just that. He will meet his wife, make a child, and learn to fire a gun.

I hate things ending with Christian. Usually, my relationships just fade or phase out until the guy realises he wants something different, something less difficult or more fulfilling than what I have to offer. Most often, I'm the one who gets my heart broken, at least on paper. It's a safer boat to be in, less holes. Better than having to live with having done the breaking. When you get your heart broken, for a time, you're perfected. Unlovable maybe, but unimpeachable. You can wallow and woe-is-me, and have the luxury of directing your hurt outward, living comfortably in your own self-righteousness.

I take the coward's approach so often I hardly realise I'm doing it – could hardly imagine another way. If you asked me if I was trying to sabotage my relationship, I'd say of course not. Though, if you got me a little drunk, I might say something different. I cheat a lot and am obvious about it. I don't answer texts from Christian when I'm out with other men. I bring men back to our apartment when he's at work in clear sight of his parents and we have loud sex. Sometimes the men leave an article of clothing in the apartment, which I then leave on display, draped over the couch or framed on the plush mauve bathmat. I leave my sound on so he can hear the little ding on my phone each time I get a new Grindr notification. We're open but I break our rules, one by one, methodically, almost as if on purpose.

When Christian breaks up with me, I'm good at acting hurt. At pretending the wind was gulped out of my lungs and make my breathing all short for him. He says I'm putting him at risk, which I argue at first is such a dweeby and cruel HIV-phobic, sex-negative bullshit argument – after all, we're on PrEP, and syphilis and chlamydia are curable, and – then I realise he's talking about his heart.

His parents refuse to make eye contact with me when I move my few possessions out of their home and into my new apartment, in the basement of a giant pre-war building in Queens at least four degrees from the original leaseholder. I snap a goodbye polaroid of Christian crying on their stoop and tack it up next to all my friends I've lost or haven't yet met, as now he joins the ranks of them, another person I'll never really know. Someone who is no longer in my life, and so is no longer. I knew what I was doing; I must have. Could see our future being laid out so cleanly. The house upstate, the domestic coupledom, his horrible job, his demand for and adoration of children, all of this sprinting forward on its inherited track into a future so undoubtably riddled with destruction and flood and violence, so impossible to conceive, a world literally burning, that instead of becoming a goddamn liar, I had to find some other way to break it.

The internet is a portal into the suffering of others — sometimes their joy, though mostly, just their suffering. The algorithms are written out to stroke discord, to point the viewer towards where it is they'll hurt the most. Sharks follow the bleeding. Traffic slows as it passes a brutal accident. Flies swarm meat. I open my computer and it breaks my heart. I close my computer. Day after day, another mass shooting, a conspiracy theory taking root in the halls of Congress and the stem of the brain, a new pipeline approved for construction, a wall on the border's built through ancestral lands, a queer Orlando nightclub becoming the site of the biggest mass shooting in the history of this country quickly followed by a Las Vegas concert overtaking that title, bombings in Brussels, immigration bans, hurricane after hurricane with late alphabet names, children in cages.

There is how the news story exists in image and in text, and then there is how that story is actually a person's entire life in sobbing and warped metal. Empathy eats you alive. You can only survive by separating these two, by reading the news and not connecting the whole wet network of human suffering to the breath you are currently taking into your lungs. And if you cannot do this, well, what else is a person to do?

My last year in New York, I let the internet tell me where to go. There are ranked lists of free things to do. The leather nights, the gear nights, the film screenings, the gallery openings, the singer-songwriter open mics, the puppet theatres, the pup parties, the play parties . . . I go to them all alone. I go to the museum performance art nights, the by-stander trainings, the DSA comedy fundraisers, the wine and paint parties – alone. Each room has its own ritual. If there's a bar, I order a cocktail, something fancy that can be milked and refilled from the flask in my pocket as I sit against the wall, surveying life like an oceanographer, some Jacques Cousteau-type with similarly dishevelled hair and aslant red beanie.

To be alone at a bar is an American rite of passage. To see everyone having their best life with friends and manage not to be lonely is to have achieved the highest state of consciousness. You can transcend the looking body simply by looking. At night, everyone is impossibly beautiful and brilliant all the time, people transformed into water, catching the light before moving on. On occasion, some of the water speaks to you, on occasion you kiss the water, go back to the water's apartment, look through the water's books and shake your head in dismay, let the water inside you. But in the end, he flows away or evaporates, so you go to a different lake or river, you go on chasing waterfalls, if you must, and order a glass of water at the bar along with your cocktail. Most nights, I won't spend more than an hour out, but occasionally when I've really transcended myself, I can stay out alone until the morning.

When Mom left us, her parents rewrote their finances to cut her out of their future deaths, which meant eventually, I will be getting her inheritance. When they sit me down at fourteen to go over the numbers, they are just numbers standing in for a gone mother and I imagine I must be set for good. After college, after my grandparents die, I do the math for myself, asking the computer, if this, then what? What's the cost of living – although never, *Why does it cost to live?* What's the average American salary for this city or that (salary, I learn, comes from the word salt (from when salt was a kind of Roman currency (the value of anything that cures meat)))? Then I subtract an eighth of it, never having needed the finer things, really. Never an especially good STEM student, I do what I can to map out the foreseeable variables – rent, eating, insurance – and then add money toward what I *cannot* see – the new funeral suit, the middle-shelf liquors mixed by the bartender herself, the potential pet lizard, etc. If I don't have any major medical problems, children, or vacations, I'll be able to live off part-time work for the next seven to ten years, give or take. When the numbers finally math out, I do a little dance, knowing full well it is a little dance of desertion. Suddenly rich and miserable, miserably rich. Every time I buy groceries, it's trading a gone woman for food. That place I first lived, half of myself, I trade in now for a new MetroCard, and she rides there on the train beside me. Every time I swipe through the turnstile, I am pulling her close enough to smell her hair. When I sign the handwritten contract for my new apartment, I am cutting off her littlest toe. Whenever I've tried to tell anyone this, they shake their head and laugh at my 'burden' – but they don't know. How heavy the groceries grow, dragging her body with me in pieces on the subway home.

There's this myth I love most about hunger. It goes: Once we were born full and stayed that way. There was a time when a body didn't need anything but what it was already equipped with. Eating was just for pleasure, an epicurean affair, savoir faire saved for evenings, for weekends, holiday parties. Inside each child was an endless well of milk, full plates of sliced beef, mustard greens. For many generations, all was good, it was all good. People lived in harmony with the world around them and the world lived in harmony right back. But things began to shift, as corruption spread like a layer of creamed cheese across the horizon that lay thick and started to grow mould. People began to please themselves all day. All day their mouths would be filled with pineapples and peaches and pheasant. They would hoard great warehouses of food and leave it to rot. And the lord, with their seven heads, looked down on all his creation stuffing their faces with pastries and meats and felt only disgust. They deemed, in their infinite wisdom and cruelty, that we must be punished for our gluttony, this invented sin, and flipped a great switch that requires us to take the world inside us in order to survive it, and so it was, and so it has ever since been.

It's late and I'm walking my body away from the one semi-gay bar in town wearing my first pair of heels. Some cute three-inch gold pumps I got for a steal from the Goodwill with no thought of the queen they belonged to before or to whom they'll be bequeathed after. And even though my dorm is normally a fifteen-minute walk away, these little steps mean it'll likely take an hour. I look elegant as a fawn wearing three-inch heels and love the slower pace they make me take. Each step forward is intentional, and I can't worry about who's looking at me and why. I hear somebody call a name that isn't mine, though I'm sure they mean me. But all I can pay any attention to is the next step in front of me, and the next, and the next.

In my gender studies class on sixties-era protest movements, we watch a documentary on the Weather Underground, a group of white kids who engaged in military-style action against the United States government. I find I'm mostly jealous of their friendships. My own friends, I can tell, are only my friends while we're here, friendships of circumstance, because we live on the same floor of our dorm, or share a class, or tried out for the same a cappella group and didn't get in. We're not particularly motivated by or dedicated towards anything. We like to drink and talk about music. We like to complain about the politics and quality of the food dining halls. In this little chrysalis, we learn to talk big and do nothing, and will come out the other side with huge and useless wings. It's not like we would ever get together to learn martial arts, or bee keeping, or bomb making. Even though we all know it's the end of the world, for some reason we believe that in whatever future there is to come, there will be wifi.

I was never a glamorous child. Always sullen-eyed and caked in mud, in ketchup. Never dressed in a dress, aside from the few times I tried on my gone mother's garments as a kid before she came back to collect them, or Dad threw the rest out. Never played with make-up. Never tried nail polish. Never batted my eyelashes seductively or pursed my lips into a mirror as if they might kiss back. Never. Each feminine gesture seemed to carry in it an unlocatable sadness. Wearing a ghost dress isn't sexy, unless . . . well, unless you're into that, and I wasn't really, although now I suppose that's all I can wear.

The first time I really try on a gown and mean it, I'm grown or grown-adjacent. For our college's annual drag event, I unearth this hideous almost wedding dress, borrowed from the theatre department's costume shop, that was last used in a production of Les Misérables worn by Fantine herself, the dress she died in night after night, the dress she killed in. It's cream with giant puffed-up sleeves. I find a wig there that looks like a beehive someone's taken a salad fork to. We learn to do our make-up from YouTube tutorials. Everyone laughs and drinks from the same cheap handle of Fleischmann's as we transform our bodies into anything else. Ericka beats my face with the concentration, if not the skill, of a professional make-up artist.

Ze likes to pretend to be an expert at anything that has to do with having a body, and who am I, really, to question? When ze finishes my look, I get up to see myself at last in the mirror, scared that staring back will be my mother, or at least me dressed in her inherited distress, or worse, how she looked in so many of the photographs that haunted our house for years, all empty-eyed and empty-smiling. But what I see instead is some whole-ass other messy bitch – me but oddly perfected and hideously bright. She's so gorgeous, I could die; I could already be dead.

Housed in the old wood gymnasium, once an old church, the student group sets up their weekly STI testing resource centre behind a foldout table. Every Wednesday, they put up painted signs that point from the student union to Wylkier Gymnasium, and it's become a bit of joke at this point for all of us on campus. If you see someone dressed slutty or just a known slutty person, you might say, *Bet they're going to Wylkier*. To a friend, it may even transform into a verb, *Did you Wylkier out this weekend or what?* And on very rare occasion, an imperative, *You better Wylkier!*

I try to go when the quad will be most populated, just after afternoon classes, and strut there like my blood's expensive. The student intern is someone I recognise from my intro to continental philosophy seminar – Jeremy, I think? He takes me into a little wooden room that looks like it might have once been a rectory and now doubles as a second girls locker room, and he asks me about my life – or more precisely, my sexual history, use of condoms, if I've ever been abused, etc. He's kind of cute, so I try to answer how I think he'd maybe like to hear. We're in a rectory, after all, so I do my best to make him smile. *Everything you say is confidential*, he tells me, and we laugh about the awkwardness of the questions on the form. He nods as if he understands everything I have to say. Is this my favourite kind of date, an intake form at an STI clinic?

Trying to impress him maybe, I tell him about the one time I sucked off some married guy 'till he yelled out his wife's name in the parking lot of the town's police station, or another story about getting fucked in an airport bathroom flying back from winter break. His eyes get a little big at that one and he leans away just slightly. Next comes the HIV test, his hands shake a little as he opens the plastic packaging and pulls out the kit. He swabs the inside of my mouth with a little white stick, rubbing up and down along the inside meat of my cheek and gums, counting down from ten. Then he gloves up to insert a needle into me and takes some blood with surprising efficacy. Nice veins he says, looking away sheepishly. I blush and then sigh a little as the elastic is released.

You'll get your results in your email in a few days, he tells me.

I drop a not-so-subtle hint about where my dorm is. Ask if I can repay him for this service, but he says that wouldn't be ethical. But he'll see me in class, he smiles.

I look forward to it, I reply, trying to seem coquettish but probably just ending up looking famished. Three days later, I follow the link in my email that tells me I have syphilis.

I've never had an STI before – or at least one that I know of. I don't feel anything though, not even like I have a cold. Being a smoker and all, and it being winter, I can't help now feeling my throat is always a little raw. Receiving the email feels like more of a rite of passage than anything else, like I'm finally entering into something promised to me – as if the disease were already written somewhere deep in my genes. You are, a voice says in my head, and you have become. I spend hours perfecting the email to the boys on campus I might have put at risk. *Dear Gentlemen*, it begins, blind cc'd to all of them. I almost don't want to go back to the clinic to get my shot of penicillin. I read about the history of the disease, how before treatment it would often lead to madness. That it gets its English name from a poem. It used to be treated with mercury, and so I imagine liquid metal spreading through me; I imagine having a skeleton of metal, and becoming indestructible as a supervillain, some hybrid between Wolverine and T-1000. In the pamphlet I get at the gymnasium, I learn one in three people will get it in their lifetimes and, if untreated, it can cause tumours to grow from the head like those hideous theatre masques. It's a small campus, so I don't know if Jeremy's heard or if he's just being a professional, but he doesn't acknowledge me in class. Even when I ask him a direct question, he offers only a single syllable reply. Whatever flicker of intrigue there might have been has clearly evaporated when faced with its possible consequence. I'm both sad and relieved it's a different student volunteer who empties the syringe of benzathine penicillin into the meat of my left ass cheek. Whitney has a more professional demeanour, like an actor playing a nurse looking over my chart through her thin oval glasses. *Stay safe*, she says after depositing the sharp into its translucent red box. *I'll see you next time, Ezra.*

As any amateur linguist or student of history can tell you, the word nostalgia was first a diagnostic term coined by a seventeenth-century Swiss medical student. From the Greek, it means to return home in pain – means the pain of returning home. It was, at the time, thought to be a proper sickness of the mind ascribed to veterans before the advent of what we've come to know as PTSD. Today, we commonly take it to mean more of a homesickness, the desire to return to what no longer exists. But this meaning can only be partially true in the face of that other earlier resonance.

The first time I come home after leaving for college, just a few months in, I have to pull over so I can throw up along the side of the interstate. Cars scream past as I dry heave before finally releasing something substantive onto the shoulder. I can't tell what it is that's made me so violently ill. I try to blame it on the box of apple cider donuts I bought at a rest stop a few miles back but know there's something else there. Memories show their pale faces as I pass old billboards. As I drive under the bridge where I smoked my first cigarette, the alley where I was first kissed, each fragment somehow exactly where I left it. I do my best to leave all my sickness back there, next to the gasoline puddle and its predictable rainbow. By the time I get back to Dad's apartment I'm almost on empty.

I was going to be early. Dangerously early, the doctors said. So they put Mom on this pharmaceutical which has since been recalled because of the danger it poses to mother and child alike, the child's heartbeat, the mother's mind. She was on two weeks of mandatory bed rest before I was big enough to be evacuated through the wound in her stomach. In those weeks, she wasn't allowed to move, even as the pills made it so she was unable to sleep. I can't imagine what kind of claustrophobic terror that would entail. It's quite common, Dad tells me, postpartum depression, following any birth, especially a difficult one. They'd both had it, in fact – his was a kind of paternal empathy response, or perhaps just his standard depression rearing up; he'd even joined a group called SADDADs – the name, from here, we can't help but laugh at. He's telling me about the pills Plath was on, newly prescribed, and the scholar who claims that this shift in dosage was what led her to kill herself. *The mind is always unstable*, he says, *in its shallow chemical bath, it responds to what you feed it*. We're sitting at the kitchen table. He's just accepted that I'm a smoker, I'm finishing up my final year of high school, and we're sitting smoking, the naked lightbulb is making ribbons above us. In response to the Plath comment, I ask, *Do you think she meant to do it – Mom, I mean – you know, the car, before she left*, stabbing out my Pall Mall in the novelty ashtray shaped like a fire alarm, the text reading, *in case of emergency, ash here*. He doesn't answer. Instead says, *Halevai*, which has become his new catch phrase whenever language won't do. We both know there isn't an answer that will satisfy. Instead, we sit in silence for a while longer. He lights another cigarette and offers me the pack.

ARNOLD: Listen, I need to talk to you . . .

ARNOLD: I want to apologise . . .

ARNOLD: Don't act like a fucking child . . .

ARNOLD: All your shit's still here. Do you want me to toss it? . . .

ARNOLD: If you want to talk, I'm around. If not, I understand. I love you . . .

ARNOLD: Coward.

I couldn't see it until it was already almost over – until it had become clear we are living through it. The winters of my childhood are gone. Proper winters. At those first demonstrations after the inauguration, the weather is almost too perfect for it to be the end of our world, beautiful spring day in the middle of winter. Seventy-six degrees. We wear t-shirts and open-toed shoes. Everyone's gathered outside the courthouse downtown, everyone's laughing and banging on pots and blowing their horns and having, in their way, a lovely time. And all I can do is shake, a thin radiator in the back of my neck hissing, building steam. All I can do is hold my breath and try not to think of what exactly we're making all this noise inside, what we're unknowingly moving in and out of our lungs. I count down from ten, and start to get lightheaded, and eventually, something biological kicks in and forces me to keep breathing.

In the 1970s, the *New York Times* published in an op-ed claiming that if we were to keep going at our current rate of production and pollution, the oceans would be dead by the year 2000. Surely, you must know we didn't slow down – in fact, quite the opposite. In 2001, my family takes a trip down to the Jersey Shore to sit on the beach, trying to get ourselves a bit of a tan, although we'll end up, as always, looking more like plastic grocery bags filled with red meat. It's the hottest week of the summer. Before Coco Chanel, a tan meant poverty and field work, but that changed once she was photographed lounging on the French Riviera, idling bepearled in magazines across America.

In the car, Mom wears her hair up in a handkerchief like a Jewish Audrey Hepburn and Dad wears a Hawaiian shirt like some fat Jew in a Hawaiian shirt. Mom's been in one of her moods, late nights at work, her days spent rearranging the refrigerator for hours on end, throwing away unexpired food and replacing it with food still sealed fresh in its packaging. So, Dad suggested we get out of Dodge for a long weekend, take our mind off our lives for a spell and escape the miserable July heat.

We arrive in Monmouth and check into our dinky pink hotel. A folding cot's been wheeled into the corner for me beneath a window that overlooks a busy side street. Since there are still a couple good hours of sun left, we drag our beach gear down to the lip of ocean. Off in the distance is the city skyline distorted, the Twin Towers almost serpentine in the heat. There are children my age and slightly older children.

There are women slathered in tanning oils, and women selling mangos and hotdogs, and beer everywhere, so much beer you could imagine it seeping up under your feet through the sand, so that if you plunged a straw into someone's sand-castle, you'd get wasted. At eleven, I'm not yet interested in such things. Instead, I collect shells and glass tumbled smooth at the water's edge, shrieking in my unchanged voice when-ever the freezing water laps my ankles. Mom brought a book and has it open on her lap, a dog-eared copy of *The Tipping Point*, but doesn't seem to be reading it, just stares out into the ocean. When I look back at them from all my assembling and curation, Dad's asleep, turning slowly and surely into a cherry red convertible, and Mom has this faraway look, like she's staring off into an ocean that's already dead.

After Arnold, a therapist tries to explain the work we're doing together. That at the root of the word psyche is soul. He says that psychology is the study of the soul, and psychiatry then is the healing of the soul. I take momentary comfort in this. But when I leave his office, I look up other common suffixes on my phone and extend this language experiment: Psychophobia is the fear of the soul. Psychometry, the measurement of the soul. Psychosepsis, an infection of the soul. Psychophilia, the love of the soul. Psychogenesis, the origin of the soul? Psychophagia, the eating of souls.

Of course, I nurse the wild narcissist in me who believes some-thing may pivot following my death. Not like an end to war or anything that grandiose, but maybe a subtler change, some minor shift in the language, maybe a progressive bill with my name attached to a list of names that stalls out in Congress. The First World War began after some Hungarian with a fancy moustache was shot. A butterfly flaps its wings in Kyoto. A fire is lit.

I choose gasoline on purpose. It's significant that it'll be a fossil fuel which returns me to dirt: what will end us all and what all this will become in another fifty million years. Everything I love, every one of us who laughs, and claps their hands off-beat, and takes asthma medicine, slowly becoming crude, becoming this thin band of subterranean petroleum in the earth's substrata. The circle, consummated. I try again and again to type out my testament for the internet, my manifesto if you must (big cringe), but all my language isn't enough, the words take on too many meanings and mean nothing all at once. All I want to be is a minor augury, the oracle at Delphi huffing fumes off the bituminous limestone. All I want to do is leave a little more room for what good people are left to do their feral blooming.

Of the ten men that make up Dad's 'minyan', there is a clear leader, and it isn't my father, thank god. A former Talmudic scholar, former Hassid, and a current used car salesman in Ossining, Itai has a magnetism that either attracts or repels – which is how magnets generally work. This is a quality necessary for any minor cult leader; they pull toward them those in need of some manner of salvation while repelling anyone who might have reasonable doubt. The one time we met, I could tell he sold cars before he'd even said anything; it was in the way he stood, as if he was trying to convince you to drive away in something shining and broken. Dad's struggled with a profound emptiness since even before Mom left, and so has found himself a man who claims to have some kind of answers, who will fill the hole with noise, if not substance. I'm not so sure of this world to believe I know which cult is more damaging than any other – the cult of capitalism, of gasoline, of reality television, of organised or disorganised religion. The cult of foodies, of political parties, of literature, of online gossip or non-profits. The men pay their dues, and eventually they all move into a converted elementary school in the woods about as far away as you can get into northern Westchester. I couldn't tell you what it is they do out there, but I like to imagine them happy. For a time, I was bitter that this group of men effectively took my father away from me, who so profoundly changed him as to be, well, no longer my father. But am I even the same person I was a week ago, let alone five years? Wasn't it me who left, who also changed? Aren't we, all of us, equally to blame?

My final therapist, in a gentle coached voice, asks me to describe my mother leaving me. Like each one before him, he is bad at pretending he isn't terribly interested in this particular life-event, for predictable Freudian reasons. Before him, I mostly told the truth, which I'd found out each time was a mistake. To name the numbness that arrived and never left. How my mom was gone off in some other life she didn't want us to be a part of and that this was sad and common as a fern. Just another kind of death, another room we walk into that cannot be entered by the living. As a child, I realised this and spoke it plainly to my therapists, but all it ever got me was furrowed eyebrows and workbooks on grief.

So with this final therapist of mine, I lie. Tell him how I was a perfected grieving subject, how I did my grieving perfectly. When she drove off, I was torn open as the ground, I say, that I stood there like a field while a backhoe loader dug a hole straight down into me. Tell him I was hurt as the earth was hurt – scarred, scared, and yet through this became sacred. Tell him the first birthday she missed I wrote a note and ate it like I was some kind of holy wall. That I felt everything very deeply. I tell anecdotes of all the appropriate ways to mourn someone leaving I've learned from films and literature. Tell him I wailed loud enough to spook the birds from their trees.

The truth is I did feel empty, only not like a grave – more like a hole you dig as a child to fill the time. How, ever since, I've been filled with time and with holes. She couldn't keep living with us, I mean really living, so she left – I understand. She gave us what she could and then had to choose her own survival.

When I speak my lie, though, in that little room filled with diplomas and offensively innocuous geometric paintings it suddenly becomes true, even brings the appearance of tears to my face which are, for all intents and purposes, real tears, not of remembered feeling but of something like relief. I know this is the last therapist I'll ever need, his eyebrows wrinkled with care and understanding, his beard nearly rabbinical, almost Robin Williams in *Good Will Hunting* before we learned he'd go on to kill himself. I cry as I describe this new history I'm inventing for myself, paint for him the child thrashing on the ground like drugged birds. Here, I am the child and the birds, and in this lie I become, at last, a good son.

At the edge of a wood that lay between two ragged settlements on what is the modern Iberian Peninsula, there was a well. But the well drew only brackish water, as the elders would tell it, so the children of the town were instructed not to drop a bucket down below, and warned of the kind of sickness that would spread inside the bodies of those who drank. One day, there was a young boy from a farther off town travelling through the wood, carrying a stack of books for Rabbi Moyshanka in a shoddy wagon behind him. He was traversing the tough terrain through the woods, rightly assuming this would be a shorter path between villages, when he came upon the well. Not knowing the stories, he lowered the bucket and pulled up the most crystalline cold water he'd ever seen. Water they write poems about. Water so clear it might as well be sky. It was only after he brought the bucket to his lips that he noticed how dark it had grown around him, how the trees appeared to be stone, how his feet were deep in mud and the only light was a thin coin suspended above him. Though it was dark, the boy could tell he was not alone. His body moved as if it were below water. There were thousands of boys there, skin bloated and no longer opaque. All looking up waiting for someone to lower the bucket into their open mouths, so thirsty to be brought back up into the light.

I wake up again in a bedroom that isn't mine. Some trick, my first thought, rare as it is I'd spend the night – or maybe it's a trick of the light. I thumb the sleep from my eyes, and look over to see no one. I reach out to make sure, and my own hand surprises me. Slenderer than the one I'm used to, cuticles a whole mess. Disgusting, I think, and try to slot in a trip to the nail salon in my head. But everything else is off a few degrees, too. The window, small and thick, looks out onto a distant winter field. Even the air enters and leaves my lungs strangely, a cleanness that cuts straight through the branches and into the blood. I reach up to find my face smooth and oval-shaped, then trace my hands downward, and there are breasts, flush, fatty, and sensitive, a new belly under my ribs and then another kind of genital. Before getting up and finding a mirror to see my face, I need to hold onto the me I know, so I slip a finger around the lip and dip an index inside, and it is as familiar and foreign as this room. Pervert, I say aloud, laughing and shaking my head, but the word comes out strange and glottal-stopped. Even though it's still dark, I hear the sounds of breakfast being prepared, eggs over the fire, and beyond that, a far off mummering in a language I somehow understand though am unable to recognise. I stand up, shivering, and find this hideous garment, a sage floral sack dress I slip over my head. I search the room for a reflective surface, finding none besides the window, which shows only my outline filled with snow and branches.

As a girl in my village, before I am expected to work, I draw stories in the dirt with my finger. I make whole books of drawings, page by page, wiping it clean as soon as I'm done, only to begin another one. Whole anthologies spill this way from my finger. Whole living cities I make and unmake with my hands. Whole new species of angels speak to little girls like me and open the doors of immaculate and metallic buildings. Sometimes the other children gather to watch as I make a bird, speak it into flight, then bury it wing-first under the soil. When I'm done, I'll make another picture and give it the gift of breathing. Sometimes I'll get quite a crowd, cheering me on as I make whole villages that disappear in the rain; though when the old men find us, they scold me with one outstretched finger, the same one I use to reinvent the world. Of course, there is no page that can hold me. I am telling more than paper can hold. Books are for dead stories, scrolls written in forgotten languages, and I'm telling what's still alive, stories that haven't been written yet and died inside the coffin binding of book covers. I'm telling stories that live for a minute on the surface of the earth, then disappear forever, back into the earth from whence they came, all with the simple movement of a hand.

I spend most days peeling and cutting potatoes and root vegetables for the town's kitchen. My sisters and I sit around the fire and laugh. Men come in, after they've finished their work in the fields or the mines, to purchase a bowl of soup thickened with cabbage and kidney, along with a thick slab of dark bread. My favourite parts of the days are here with my sisters, before the men arrive. A man named Levi is often trying to speak with me, like he wants something, and the urgency of that wanting makes my neck tremble in disdain. He has nice hair, my sisters say, so I say it's true as well, though nothing moves inside me when we speak. His hair is long and straight as the mane of a well-groomed show pony. When we speak it is always cold and cordial as a knife. Transactional as a bill of sale, well-thumbed. A recipe handed down. Love is meant to be different, though, isn't it? I've always imagined there'd be a quickening in the chest. You look at a man and it should put the wind back into you. A flock of birds should lift off at once from the surface of the water, not flap there desperately in the lake, then drown.

I want more, but what is there to want and where is there to go? The city's a week away by foot and the road's impossible through the winter and much of spring. And what would I even do when I got there? Who would I become? Would I leave my sisters behind to bear this life without me? Even Rachel, whom I used to kiss as a girl, is married now and refuses to be alone with me. There are many ways to grow old before your time. I suppose I could keep refusing or just go ahead and find myself a man whom I can find tolerable. Which is more than most get and less than anyone deserves.

I end up taking a man because this is what is expected of me. Levi is fine. He's the butcher's son, which my sisters find very impressive, though, for me, he is just a man who always has to wash the blood off his hands. I take this man who was raised to look at an animal in pieces. And, sure, we get our fair share of good meat, but what is life to a man who sees the world this way – as a living thing waiting to be disassembled, one that can be separated by nothing but a blade? Levi is sweet to me, and I do my best to be acceptable. I do my wifely duties; I make his bed and his children. I hum as I pin up our laundry to the sky. I go cook with my sisters. I want more from this life, but the only example I see is the one the gentiles show us – the women, in their elaborate gowns, gorgeous women being pulled in carriages behind horses, so delicate they must be kept up above the mud. And maybe that's a trap as well, isn't it? To be a caged bird, so precious you don't even know the dirt.

When it comes time for it, how would you run?

My eldest is a nogoodnik, and I love him for this. He lies all the time, for no good reason. *Where were you, Herschel?* I might ask, and he goes on to spin a yarn about lying down in a field while watching giants swat warplanes out of the sky. *What did you learn at school today, Herschel?* and he'll talk about how babies are born pulled from the earth by their hair like turnips. What is a lie anyway but the imagination at work? He is a mess of brown tangles, always filthy, regardless of when he was last bathed. It might be a problem when he gets older, when he becomes the type of man who might trade his shoes for wine, but I don't worry just yet; don't want to squash his dreaming. This way, at least, he might lie enough to be able to imagine a life outside of here.

Everywhere I live is beside highways. You grow so used to the sound, it gets to the point where you can't sleep without cars churning concrete in the near distance, without that dull roar and dank perfume of petroleum. Like that thing they say about waterfalls – though, never having lived by one myself, I can't confirm. Route 90, 80, I-35. Behold, the asphalt snake wrapped around the belly of the world. Concrete stretching out in every direction, tethering the past to the future, holding the globe in place. A little cross-section of America on its way to America. At night, I imagine who's at the wheel. All of them at once, once and for all.

The project of the interstate began in the fifties under the guidance of Dwight D. Eisenhower, same man who named the military–industrial complex. Same military–industrial complex that, in partnership with the automobile industry, sold the idea of individual freedom housed inside the belly of a car. And, in this way the government, colluding with several extractive profit-driven industries, took up the holy doctrine of the interstate.

All this hums past my window each night and into the early morning. Thousands of people passing through a slim bath of mechanical light. A rig, with a man smoking at its helm, pulling no cargo. A woman spilling her coffee on the way to a night shift at the hospital. A vanity licence plate reading hmw0rd. A group of teens speeding fast toward Providence.

I'm both my parents the night I'm conceived. It's been seven months since our wedding. I've just stopped taking my birth control, and we've long since decided to quit with condoms. We'll see, we say, never expecting how fast seeing will come. We met in our MA programme at Hunter in a course on futurist literature. Not every imagining of the future, we learned, is utopian. Often, it's the fascists who plot the best, who lay the most meticulous plans of rats and men. I love how she always had something cutting to say, eyebrows narrowed under that messy crown of reddish-brown curls; and him, I didn't notice at all until he approached me after class to ask me to lunch. We lied to her parents, pretended we weren't living together. We taught high school and couldn't imagine raising a child in the city on that salary, but never worried about it until we had to. The night's almost non-eventful. I put on a Sly record while, across the room, I light some candles. When he slips inside me bare for the first time, I feel every inch of us worry.

In 1897, French sociologist Émile Durkheim theorised four different types of suicides – the egoistic, the altruistic, the anomic, and the fatalistic –

I love how sure and clear these words sound. I love anything that breaks suffering down into a clean taxonomy you might look to when lost and nod your head in the performance of understanding.

For much of my life, I've misunderstood the concept of the death drive, thinking it means, as one might, living as though you've already died. Quentin, a psychology major, corrects me. He also tells me that Freud didn't believe there is a singular drive, but multiple, plural as a braid that makes up the shape of our lives. He says the death drive manifests as aggression, compulsion, and self-destruction, and is the opposite of eros. I haven't told him I cheated on him yet. A lot. Is eros really the opposite of the death drive? I wonder what the drive toward nothingness would be? Toward becoming an open pit? A billboard swallowed by kudzu? A stone angel beaten into a new shape by rain?

Anne Sexton blurbed Hughes's book *Crow*, writing: *Let all the poets of the world bow down their heads in admiration and awe.*

A week before her dear friend Sylvia died, Sexton writes the poem 'Wanting to Die'. Ten years later she takes her own life, in her own idling car.

egoistic, altruistic, anomic, fatalistic

I wonder why all of the Google searches that come up when you type in 'Wanting to Die' are resources for how to stay alive.

With the man still asleep, I write a note and slide it into my pocket. I write it in wet ink using one of his bespoke fountain pens, so the text smears into near illegibility soon as I fold it:

I see my hands in front of me, gripping the wheel. They look strange, separate from myself somehow, like watching someone else play an arcade game. The white lines in the road look almost pixelated in their straightness. Something unlocatable pilots the body that pilots the machine. This car's a plastic and metal cage that eats gasoline same as it eats women. I have to leave here one way or another. My husband is singing nasally and off-key:

> *His mind was blown out of his car / the lights the lights*
>   *the lights*
> *the lights had changed*

My son is in the backseat rolling his eyes so far back they're almost entirely white. He looks possessed.

There's nothing in front of me.

I see myself ahead of myself, as if I'm watching the lag on old VHS tape. See myself lifting up the canister and bathing the figure in the red sweatshirt, the scent floods the senses before dressing the figure in flames. For a moment, it looks like huge white wings are wrapped around him.

Fifteen protests this month. Each one, like poetry, makes nothing happen, it survives. I watch us yell at cops, knowing they aren't the politicians who militarised their funding, or funded their militarisation, who are themselves just figureheads for systems that will continue their funeral march well after our little deaths. We know those who profit most off of suffering are not here, they are floating above the world in private jets, in their penthouses that pierce the clouds in this dystopian novel they've made into real life. Yet here we are. Everything stands in for a kind of violence elsewhere. The first rule of semiotics. To fix anything here on earth, we must first tear the page. What else can be done with my one precious and terrible life?

The book is sitting on top of Dad's old roll-top desk, almost theatrically lit, the cover is some material that doesn't reflect back light. I'm young still, and am not supposed to go into his study, even when he's not working there. I wear my red winter socks so as not to make any noise, approach it slow, how one might a frog, from behind. I can see the cover's written in some odd alphabet, Hebraic but not quite – something older, no accents. The book pulses and I leap back when I see the pages almost breathing, like there's something on the other side trying to get out. I reach slowly down to peel back the cover only to find the pages blank, so I write my name, then step back fast as the book starts its pulsing again. Lying open on its back, the book takes one deep breath and then, all at once, insects begin chewing up through the page with my name on it, more and more of them start pouring out into the room.

I flee just before the revolution. Before our names can be pulled off any ledger. You can see it in the wind, the way history is moving, and so I, from a family adept at reading the wind, decide to get out of the way of history. We've only been in this country a few generations anyway, and it was as bad for us here as it was anywhere else. I got the job at the factory because my father sold the fat from his butcher shop there and put in a good word. We produce soap. What could be more boring than soap? They cart in the animal fat in large wooden boxes. You can smell it even before it gets to the gates, almost biblical in its stench – one of those ancient sicknesses, a river overflowing with dead fish. My job is to break down the crates and then shovel the gelatinous stank into large metal drums, which are then processed by men in gloves. I am not given any gloves for my shovelling. This is my duty, day in and day out – my daily bread, shovelling fat – and soon, I have developed one particular set of very unattractive muscles in my right shoulder, arm, and back, making me stand like a lop-sided, rain-bloated tree. Half strong man, half spoiled cream. At night, I use the very soap we make at the factory to wash the rotten blood from underneath my fingernails. What sort of life is this for a man in love with books? Who himself would have chosen a path in books, if not for all the god in it? My wife won't touch me anymore because of this godforsaken smell. Then again, she's too tired from teaching schoolchildren all day anyway. I've never been a joyful man, but still, how sad and perfectly ordinary to be another person to whom history simply happens.

My mother invented such wild stories for me as a child that, now that I'm a man, I can't stand to stay in this cold and simple country. She spoke of cities where buildings grew taller than trees. Where, at their peak, behind walls of glass, you could bathe in a hot bath of water. She spoke of citrus. Told me about metal horses that lined streets paved with stones so flush they appear to be one perfectly carved rock. She was a gloomy woman, I could always see, though of course she never spoke of it directly. All Jews are sad, she'd say; sadness, our birthright. She abided my father – dumb man whose only passion was his business, the business of cutting up animals – and tolerated him in his stupidity. At night, she would whisper these stories of the world outside our small town, places where you didn't have to drag water to your house for drinking, didn't have to live in fear of men with swords, didn't have to wear the same clothes, day in and day out. Of course, this was well before the men came to our home on horseback, before the real butchery began to spread across the country. She had premonitions, I guess, of what was to become of us. And so her stories were never of here, but always elsewhere, all of them whispering in their subtext, whispering just below the surface: *run*.

Flee is such an ugly word, really. Brims with cowardice. I prefer the word *flight*, which has a strength to it, an orientation, defies gravity. I hide for two days buried in straw in the bottom of a ship bound for America before this becomes unbearable. All my ghosts are trapped in here with me, but I'm good at ignoring them. I think little of the family I'm leaving behind, only of the stench of this damned straw as it grows more putrid, partially digested, Old Testament wet. They won't throw me overboard so long as I earn my keep, so I keep my mouth shut as I wash their cups and plates. I am young and shouldn't have been married at this age anyway. This was what they wanted me doing all day, shovelling fat out behind the soap factory? Would they one day promote me to the esteemed position of being allowed to work myself to death indoors? Saving up a year's salary to buy shoes for my son? No. What I want most is to sit somewhere and read, to have the time to paint with simple colours, but of course it would be my god who made me colour-blind. It's not so bad, really, being a coward, if it means being alive.

Impossible to describe what months at sea does to the body to someone who hasn't lived it. Hasn't had all their senses reoriented to the nature of water. The body begins to lie to itself, says all the world is water and has always been, that dry land is a myth made up to scare children. The stomach unhinges, becomes a useless barometer. The eyes focus the best they can on any fixed place only to have the body remember nothing is ever fixed, even the horizon. I stand for hours on the deck of the ship smoking until the cigarettes run out, and do my best to settle on a fixed point and stare into it. What I would give to see land again. What would happen? Will I remember how to walk on it without toppling over? Will I grow nostalgic for the ocean? The instability of even the most basic tenets of gravity. Some people are bred for water, come from a water people. But me, I'm bred for bread – what comes out of the earth has always been my currency. My mother used to tell stories of the sea, but she always drew them in the dirt with her finger, and that is where I come from. Of a place and out of place at once. The horizon, not unlike death, is the point beyond which all perception fails, the other side of which is unimaginable. When up on deck someone at last calls out land, I know this is what they must mean. Look there, brethren, behold off in the distance, there lie the limits of our imagination.

EZRA: Sorry for ghosting.

ERICKA: . . .

EZRA: SORRY !!

ERICKA: it's been like six months asshole.

EZRA: Idk, I've been sad.

ERICKA: everyone's sad dude.

EZRA: Ya but I been like reallllly sad. Tho I feel like things might be starting to look up.

ERICKA: o good. happy for you. i'm still pissed.

EZRA: You been alright?

ERICKA: no bitch, of course not.

I go to Nowhere to watch the election results. It's supposed to be a party. The bar's got everyone dressed out like sluts, or maybe there isn't any theme for the evening and folks have just dressed for their own internal occasion. As the night wears on, though, and the results begin coming in, you can feel the bottom drop out of the tiny dance floor. Slowly the music fades and we're all just standing there, in our underpants and harnesses, floating over an empty pit and no one is speaking. A group of us spill out front, still in our jockstraps and leather, grateful for the sudden shock of cold, as we smoke and glare at the gutter. Gutted. I've never been more naked. I buy a slice of pizza but don't taste it, barely feel the cheese burn the roof of my mouth. One by one, people leave the bar, alone or in pairs, searching for some comfort. I venture back inside to retrieve my clothes, slowly dress myself out in the cold, and walk my body off to wander these streets. Couldn't possibly go home to be alone with myself in my apartment with all those ghosts, to twitch and pace in circles in my apartment in my head. Instead, I walk past ground-floor windows, and it's comforting to hear all the people plotting in hushed tones or sobbing. When I make my way down to the subway platform, everyone's looking down over the platform edge at the rats who don't know anything is different, who will one day inherit all this. The whole city in mourning, bent-necked, cut stems, drooping flower heads. I tongue the new wound at the roof of my mouth and thank the pain for keeping me grounded here.

I watch an old man with a crook and a dog herd his modest flock down Nostrand, right in the middle of the street. They pass through cars unseen. There are maybe twenty of them, ragged things, passing the Burger Kings and panaderias. If you get close enough, their eyes look like stab wounds in stretched canvas. I reach out to touch one, and his wool is thick and warm against my hand, as if holding onto some far-off sunlight. It turns to snap at me with its big yellow incisors, so I step back and watch the flock pass slowly through the city.

People die and leave behind their libraries. A lifetime of collecting books and they all say peace with no plan for them. I apply on a whim and find work at this used bookstore on the Lower East Side. I work there for my last year, longer than any job I've held, or any relationship for that matter. I'm frankly surprised the guy hired me, with no experience, connections, or charisma. Every former English major wants a bookseller job in New York – until, of course, they find out what it pays.

One of my duties at the shop is to answer the phone (which I'm horrible at, thanks to the common phobia of my generation) and make notes for our book buyer. Twenty boxes of rare surgical textbooks, one box of Dutch and German language literature, a whole basement of cheap paperback mysteries. Each time, I write a little note for Lukas so he can call back and we can arrange a time for them to come into the store, or, if it's worth it, we'll drive to them in his little white van. Generally, the people on the phone are exasperated, and you can hear the grief curdle slowly to disdain when they begin to think I'm trying to scam them. No one can believe how worthless their loved one's libraries are. A whole wall of books representing a lifetime of deep study and care might only math out to a hundred sweaty dollars in their pocket. I vow here and now never to leave behind anything that someone else will have to worry over, to lose sleep or money on.

My boss looks like he was born in this store, his hair shock-white even as a child, which you can see in the picture on the desk taken in some long-abandoned countryside. If you were to draw a sharp-angled German man from your most brutal imagination, he might look like Lukas. He's owned this store since the eighties, a shotgun layout with old books piled up to the ceiling loosely organised by invented genre: *The collected works of deviant gods. Myths & facts. The poetry of gone places.*

My other duties are to catalogue and alphabetise; to greet people as they walk in and then wish them well as they inevitably walk out, usually without buying anything; to proffer a disapproving look if anyone should slip an old volume into their jeans or pocketbook, though nothing more than that, just a look. Whoever's going to steal a book, I think, likely really needs it. Once, a kid came back with an illuminated copy of the Quran he'd swiped weeks ago to say, *Sorry, I was in a lot of pain and just needed to take something beautiful.* I tell him to keep it.

I like it best in the morning, when the store is empty and the light hits the front window just so, all the dust is illuminated into sharp, barely moving lines, and I can read a beautiful sentence, forget I've read it, and then read that same sentence again.

Walking through Crown Heights, I triple-check the outline of the phone in my pocket, to make sure I'm not slipping. Little glass and metal fetish rooting me to the present. I can, if I want, pull up photographs of this neighbourhood from a hundred years back and see the same people dragging their children behind them on their walk to shul. Out of place, I pull out the little glass face to snap a selfie or text someone living. Sometimes, I reach for my phone, and it's there in my pocket; other times, it's empty and I feel only the outline of my tzitzit.

We don't carry new books, and it's best this way. There's so much pageantry around new literature, especially in New York. It's nice to have a little refuge for the largely forgotten titles. To be reminded that even the most glamorous and lauded books, praised to the moon and beyond, will disappear from memory only to haunt the shelves of some secondhand store like ours. A sanctuary, if you will. Where all the circus elephants go to retire and live out their slow days in peace, no longer having to perform for anyone. Even the big books, books that once gripped the country's imagination, that were made into popular films and reprinted bearing the faces of famous actors, or led to an assassination or made headlines as the celebrated memoirs of great and gone men, now languish on shelves beside their unknown contemporaries, ancestors, and grand-children, waiting desperately to be picked up, to be touched and looked at by anyone. Writers who were giants, spoken about once as if they'd stand firm against the test of time, also succumbed to time, only to stand upright now, spine out, at a height you'd need a ladder to reach, some having occupied their shelf for the better part of a tenth of a century. In the slow hours, I try to visit with them, keep them company, part their hair and rub oil into their backs. I imagine it's lonely to have once been so praised only to now be almost entirely ignored. Are they better off, the ones who only ever had a small cadre of dedicated readers? Maybe it's worse, having been loved? *Good morning my pretties*, I say, when I unlock the door in the morning and hear them all reply back, each one in its own retired and exhausted register.

One day, during my final year of high school, a boy in my town burned alive in his car on his way to school. He'd been drinking. I'm sitting in an AP History class when it happens and won't learn about it until later that night. In class, we're discussing the ethics of war, what might constitute justifiable murder, the moral backbone of collateral damage. At the suicide prevention assembly the next day, the choir performs an arrangement of 'My Heart Will Go On'. They still had it ready to go from our last grief assembly. We hear that Céline Dion standard spill from the same twenty-five mouths five separate times that year – even though of course it won't, the heart, I mean, go on.

Most often, we get books dropped off in gross plastic shopping bags, or I'll discover a few bankers' boxes left as donations outside the door in the morning. There's the occasional professional antiquarian bookseller who'll come in with a duffle bag of sellable books taken from estate sales and store closures. It's clear, in how they speak and handle the texts, that they do not love the books, that money has transformed them into any other kind of currency. A woman in an actual mink coat and tight black plaits grows impatient while we assess her books – she's selling a collection of Loebs, common titles, *The Phaedrus*, some Seneca – and is predictably pissed that we've offered less than she might have gotten from the used book emporium down the street. Why, I wonder, is someone in a five-thousand-dollar coat worrying about thirty dollars in cash? But then you can see the way she looks at them, laid out there on the table, they aren't books at all. There is only the body of the dead man she's lost, laid out in his green and pristine dust jacket. A brother, perhaps, who left on his own terms, terms no one else will understand. She is seeing his hand slowly peel back the cover of the great dialogue we've just offered her one dollar and fifty cents for even as he is perhaps finally off somewhere, conversing with the dead philosopher himself. But, in truth, it wouldn't matter how much we offered – no money is going be enough to bring him back into the room with us. A stray tear disrupts her flawless makeup, and she blinks hard, mad at her own salt, says *fine*, holding the cash like a spray of flowers meant to cover the stench of death.

My favourite customers are the ones who spend their years reading and reselling books here, using their store credit to purchase more books. To those people this is no different from a public library, and it's what I like best about the shop – how, during the best of times, it can feel as if we exist outside of money and outside of time.

I find myself walking, as I often do when I can't sleep, and I can't ever seem to sleep anymore. The city is mostly quiet at night, or the town is silent with people asleep in their beds, or the desert is freezing around me, so I bundle up in all my layers against the cold. Wherever I am, I keep a fire going in my hand; breathe the fire in to keep it alive. Hum to myself some manner of song, and I carry the song and flame with me as I walk, the night like an old coat around me. The landscape slowly unrolls as I pass through it all like a pointer moving across a line of text, right to left then back again, attempting to maintain some lie of linear movement. All the creatures come out at night to glare at me or shake my hands. Strangers approach for a cigarette. I share what I have with them, knowing there will always be another pack.

On rare occasions, we'll go pick up buys in Lukas's van. Anything over twenty boxes is worth a trip if it promises to fill out one of our depleted sections. The ride there is largely in silence, and I'm surprised each time how different the city looks from up high – even the most minor adjustment is enough to change your whole perspective. Occasionally, he'll point to a street corner and recount a memory, often something from the mid '80s, adjacent to someone pseudo-famous and long dead and generally gone from the public imagination. For him, as for anyone who lives long enough, street corners become haunted places.

In this way I get to see inside so many New Yorks; every apartment is a little portal into someone's vanquished or vanishing life. I'm always silent while Lukas talks and hands over the envelope of cash. My job is to haul the boxes to the elevator, or worse, and more often, down the three to five flights of stairs, pausing occasionally to dry heave on a landing, reconstitute, and continue on. Someone is leaving the city for an old folk's home after living in this one-bedroom apartment for thirty-five years. Someone's aunt passed away in her sleep, and here are the remains of her life, scattered around us among the perfume bottles and antique musical theatre posters. Someone's brother hanged himself in the kitchen, and here is the library he stared at as he swung. The apartment is otherwise empty, and I wonder if this is how sparely he lived or if maybe they've already carted out the rest of him. All these lives boxed up and in transition, all these lives here in the layers of dust, gathering like children atop all they've read and kept. I can feel all of them in my knees and lower back as I carry them down to the truck.

After someone threatens to murder me at the laundromat, I decide to take the day off work. It's a privilege, I know, to be able to call in sick, to lie and be believed. He was upset at something, the man, yelling at someone else for who knows what reason, some imagined or real breach of etiquette. Then, when he couldn't escalate any further without it becoming a felony, he pivoted his rage outward, widening his lens, and threatening to murder every person in here, of whom it was only me and that other guy. *I'll kill every single one of you faggots.* Which is how I know I'm being addressed. And though I leave my headphones in, it's clear I've heard him, that I'm conscious of having been hailed. I skip folding my clothes and stuff them quick into the bag while he gets right up in my face, smelling like the opposite of a laundromat. I prepare to be stabbed, steady my breathing so I can take the blade. *It'd feel so good to murder you*, he says, as I hoist the bag over my shoulder, so close to my ear I feel his breath inside me as I slide past, pretending all I can hear is music, Debussy or someone else who died long before the invention of the industrial washing machine. Someone who, in the pursuit of true music, couldn't be bothered with all this noise. I'm ready somehow – ready for the blade – and surprised the thought of dying makes me neither sad nor panicked, nor even particularly pain avoidant. Incidents of violence have increased everywhere, surprisingly or not, even in this city. When I get home, I fold my still-damp clothes slowly. Drape what I can over the radiator, over the cabinet knobs, and bookshelves. I do my 'good person' task of trying to empathise with this man, now that I'm a safe enough distance away, but realise I know nothing about him except how he was dressed and his temporary penchant for ambient violence. In the end, I come to the conclusion that he must have had his reasons, that likely I deserved it, and for some reason none of that makes me feel any better.

Amazon Page Description: *Z'Rebs Miraculous Waters*

Remember the flood? You survived it. You were on a boat, floating over a flooded planet. That was you. Water has the power to destroy as water has the power to cleanse, to make holy. Remember when the prophet struck his staff to a rock and out from it poured crystal clear water? You were there, you gaped in amazement as solid rock opened to make way for life itself. What makes life possible if not the clarifying properties of water? And what are we made of mostly, if not 60 per cent water, 30 per cent meat, and 100 per cent God? Tell me, where have you been all these years, brother? These waters were cultivated from a sacred well, blessed by a man of God in every tongue left, all the holiest of the holies, if you get my drift. Clean off that dirt! Remember how you wandered for generations through the desert? This is the liquid life-stuff we carried inside us all along. Trust me and the other elder Maggids of Ephratah, NY. If you order now, it comes with an accompanying prayer scroll and ball cap. Start getting your life, your life, back into the old order of things.

After Mom leaves, our house descends into a makeshift shiva. We stay home from school, Dad covers the mirrors, and we sit low to the ground, though obviously there is no body here. There is nobody here. Of the many kinds of grieving, we happen to be saddled with one where we, Dad and me, clearly weren't enough – and where else could the fault lie? Whenever people do come over, they bring us fruit baskets and all the wrong language:

I'm so sorry . . . She loved . . . It's a shame . . . I remember . . . It's okay . . .

What I return to most often is a sense of numbness. How many of my days have been dense grey fogbanks? For twenty years, I smoke every evening. And there's the stretch of time where I live in that shallow hammock of opiates, cradling me close like a new wet lamb. I won't say it ruled my life or ruined it, but they were a daily ritual, blank little holidays, chasing disembodiment – and now, as I swipe through what was and what might have been, so much of the urgency is replaced by a kind of haze I curated as a way to survive my own mind. I tried to make my life what I hoped death might look like, a weighted blanket, the arms of a comforter wrapping around you as you watch your own story unfold across a screen outside of you. But, of course, I realise now, death is quite the opposite. It is reliving all of it, the fog become sentient, whatever's left, feeling every inch of the needle work its way in, then out again, and then back in. The mark you leave on the world, left forever in you.

Amazon Reviews: *Z'Rebs Miraculous Waters*

Smells amazing! This is a great hair refresher and really helps to revive yesterday's style

Great. Light. Refreshing. Scalp feels great.

Muy buen producto, deja el pelo con buen volumen que dura hasta el próximo lavado y no deja.el pelo tieso, se siente liviano, lo volveré a comprar, es muy bueno y he probado muchos otros

I have fine limp hair. This adds just the right amount of volume. Love this!

It gives good volume . . .

Be aware of size. 1oml tiny packets. Very tiny.

I'm so mad ☺ this is a fake

I love this. I add a little bit of Myrhh and Peppermint oil to it.

It works

The precise moment I leave my body, I am being lifted. Transferred from the stretcher to the hospital bed. It's telling we haven't invented a new method for this old inexorable act, that we still rely upon the technology of hands to do our lifting. Even today, with our mapped genomes, telehealth, and laser surgeries, we still depend on hands lifting a body from one bed to another. There's comfort there. That some things are already perfected or imperfectible.

The laying of hands is a Christian rite that can ordain clergy or pass on belief or bless the spirit. It's antecedent in Judaism, called Semikhah, means the passing of Torah and represents an unbroken chain of tradition. At my bar mitzvah, which I hated, we did this by passing the scroll from my grandmother to my dad to me, and I hefted the thing above my head, almost the same size as my torso, before spreading it out to read, or rather recite from memory and pretend to read, the story of a man trapped inside a whale. The underlying moral: god sees you, everywhere. This wasn't clear to me in the moment, of course, but now I can only think of all touch this way. As the words worked their way through me, they were made new – generations of touch spilling out my mouth.

This happened in a village near what is today Utena. Every winter, the nights would grow longer than a sentence spoken by a grandmother turning soup. It wasn't clear whether time had lost its sense or if God had simply fled the village for better weather. The temperature dropped low as a fieldmouse trembling in the undergrowth, hiding from owls. Every winter, the village boys, one by one, would stand guard with a lantern on the high wooden outpost, beside them a bell and a knife. Each boy's mother would wrap a cooked fish in newsprint for him to eat. Were he to see anything coming from the wood, he was meant to ring the bell and cast his blade into the darkness to keep the darkness at bay. Most nights, nothing. But every awful once in a while would come a ringing from the blackness followed by a scream and this heaviness would drag its muttering lashes and sobbing wind past their windows. The village would wake the next day to an empty outpost as the next boy would be asked to step into that covenant. Some winters no boys were taken. Other years, six. Come spring, the town would assemble to etch the names of children into the walls of their synagogue and for a time these names protected those who prayed inside. And this is how it was, season after season, until one spring soldiers came from the capital with their railroad. The village became a place between cities. The railroad brought milk, and wool, and strangers. The strangers came with computing machines, with crucifixes carved from pig-bone, with novel illnesses, and knives shaped like genitals. And all was good, as the people of the village marvelled at their new prosperity, drinking thick bone-broth at every meal. Many winters passed without incident beneath their new electric lamps. And under this illumination, the boys grew proud and cruel, gathering in packs like dogs. They were blood clotting in the streets. Everyone suffered when they passed. It wasn't until the government collapsed and the railroad failed and there wasn't enough to eat, that blame came back hungry to the village. When winter returned it remained dark all year. Dark as the inside of a crow's egg. Dark as stones in the place of eyes. Amphibious dark. Rat-jizz dark. Cataclysm dark. When daylight finally returned, it found the village empty as a bell with its tongue cut out. The grounds were covered in fish bones. The synagogue, knifed through with our names.

It's coming faster now. One city bleeds into another. I don't notice at first. On the subway, you'll already hear a dozen different languages spoken just sitting there, and sometimes it's a hundred years between stops. But I make a right onto Fifth, and the avenue is a great expanse of water, and there in the distance, a little boat filled with every living animal. I hear the accelerant sloshing around, heavy in my bag. Blink and the street's returned, but there are only men arguing over the price of bread, book shops on every corner. Blink and there's that herd of goats moving down the street slow as handwriting, a fleet of matte grey Cadillacs. A man wrestles an angel only to kiss him on the mouth. The riot cops have moustaches and are dressed clean as prison guards in the camps. I look down at my phone and find only a prayer book. I tear the skin of my hands punching the wood door of the closet again and again, and Arnold won't let me out. I hear the crowd in the distance, singing 'Zog Nit Keynmol', as one by one their voices fall away, and when they finally come into view, I see person after person falling silent under a soldier's bayonet. Every bank window I walk past is stained glass and breaking, every past is stained with banks, and behind those windows all my dead walk beside me.

EZRA: I had a dream about you

ERICKA: sex dream?

EZRA: You wish ☺ .

ERICKA: what'd i do

EZRA: We were kind of just sitting around in this old mansion, but one that had gone to seed.

ERICKA: grey gardens?

EZRA: Exactly, and all our food grew out of the cracks in the walls and we just ate grains and flowers, and it seemed like the world had ended outside, so we wandered these massive empty rooms searching for something desperately but couldn't name exactly what it was.

ERICKA: sounds like a nightmare.

EZRA: No, it was paradise.

Since I'm not on any listservs and move around a lot, I find out about the reunion late on the alumni page, when everyone's already planning on going. When I click 'attending', Ericka reaches out to see if I really am, if I want to room together, and can I believe it's been five years? We joke about being old. They've been living in London on an artist fellowship sponsored by some ancient colonial university and are teaching the undergrads there how to make sculptures out of trash. They've been making site-specific experimental hybrid film/sound installations built out of reclaimed garbage, which I've been seeing online and have to assume the full effect doesn't translate well over the screen – at least, I hope not. They haven't much kept in touch with anyone else from school either. Neither of us is sure we even want to go. Who actually chooses to step into the past like that if it can be avoided? Memory should come up when it does, and no more often than that. Better to live one's life in the present without directly taunting the ghosts, inviting them in. I say I will, though. I don't have much else going on, and, well, there's a hole that needs filling, maybe I'll be able to find someone to help fill it. And maybe it won't be so bad.

On the commuter train up to campus for the first time since fleeing, all the news is about fires. Not the ones set by protesters but the kind the earth gives back to us. On our phones, we all see the skies above California turned orange as if a desert was lifted and placed up there in the heavens. Southern California to the Bay Area lying under a thick blanket of burnt citrus and everyone's holding up their phones to take pictures instead of running to find a place they can breathe. This is all you need to know about the end of our species I think, what supersedes the desire to survive is the desire to look, to document the world as it leaves us. In my notebook, I cross California off my list of places to flee to. Then I draw the flat earth and slash two lines through it.

By the time I arrive on the campus, I realise it will indeed be 'so bad'. I start shaking uncontrollably in the short Uber from the station as we approach the arch welcoming us back to the college. It's a perfect untouched arcology, a mausoleum, preserving all my various memories exactly where I left them, frozen in space in the meat of my brain. Before even checking in and dropping off my bags, I follow someone into my old freshman dorm and break down sobbing in the lobby. Co-eds pass silently around me looking on in horror at this sad old man weeping in their new home. Some sophomore RA approaches and asks, *You okay, sir*, in a voice that's clearly terrified of what I may do. I look up from myself at his youth, his new experimental moustache, and watch as he tries to gather up all his authority into his thin voice. But before he can ask me to leave, I say to him, *I used to live here, and even then, I didn't live here*. And feeling how ridiculously melodramatic that sounds, I start laughing, then start laughing-laughing, chaotic laughing, the sound catches in my throat and cycles there. He backs away slowly, eyes widening in fear.

Little has changed over these five years aside from how the kids dress – more monochromatic dark academia – and the technology – more people staring deeply into their phones, more security and surveillance in the dormitories. Other than that, exactly how I left it. Except when I pass the closet where I sucked my first collegiate dick only to find it's been bricked over, and remember too, the boy's dead – overdose. I can't believe I'd forgotten him until this new wall excavated that old memory. Everywhere I look, something I've forgotten raises its head to grin back at me. At the gazebo, Quinten smokes his first cigarette from my pack, looking at me like I mean something and won't hurt him. Ericka holds back my weirdly long and greasy bangs so I can vomit cleanly in the basement of the student centre. At the side of the library, I'm bent over a book reading Yoko Ono scores out loud to a gallery of laughing friends. Over there in the quad, another dead kid does a handstand to try to impress my group before they come over to introduce themself.

It's a harrowing realisation that people continue to live their lives even when you're not looking directly at them. You learn object permanence and then forget it. In my mind, everyone is exactly who they were where I left them. A bit of a hybrid narcissism/psychosis situation, I know, but maybe it's also a kind of a gift as well, that in my head everyone remains young with decent skin and their whole future in front of them. This illusion collapses in on itself at the dance in the barely renovated gymnasium, when suddenly – there everyone is. A few of them I've watched grow over the years online, others are half-known to me, a vaguely recognisable chin or T-zone, while still others have fallen entirely off my grid, emerging from the waters of the past with a receded hairline, a wife, and screaming infant. The crust-punk anarchist now working for the State Department. The burnout in the leather jacket who sold molly for me to take with my theatre professor, now a social worker in Pittsburgh. All the theatre kids who are still trying to make it in the theatre. All the queers and radicals who re-closeted or chose something easier. All the people who married their college sweethearts. I'm embarrassed by how many of them have remained in touch.

Quinten is there with his husband. Both of them look rich, wearing matching tuxedos with uncreased neon high-tops. He introduces me and his husband's eyes narrow into sickles like, *Oh, so this is that little bitch?* And although I can't for the life of me remember exactly what it is I did, I'm sure I did it, and sure I deserve this. So I just smile and shake his hand a bit too enthusiastically, then pretend to see a friend across the gym. They're playing music from five years ago that's sadly already nostalgic, M.I.A. and Crystal Castles, and we've assembled around us the group that seems to have the least strong college ties and pass my bottle of whiskey around like we used to, pretending it's novel, that it isn't something we all still do. Almost everyone avoids talking about the new president. The few who do are grandstanding and annoying. Everyone acts like they knew it was coming, like they have such acute political vision, that this is just an extension of the same terror that America always was, and it is of course – and of course it isn't. How much of this affectation is wanting to feel superior to the nightmare we all have always lived in, to have known, so you don't have to be shocked by being taken advantage of by the unknown?

Someone whose name I can't recall but took a film class with (Janine?) asks me how I've been, and I get overwhelmed having to account for my life. How do you sum up five years so as to appear of value? What's the currency and tenor of this dialogue? Where have all my social graces gone? *I work at a bookstore*, I reply, but offer nothing more, and this seems to satisfy her, at least enough to move on to address someone more interesting.

Everyone is better dressed than I am, wearing suits that fit their bodies. It's supposed to be a formal function I realise now that I'm here, wearing a black hoodie, black cutoff jean short-shorts, and a blond bobbed wig. Everyone is laughing about some meme I haven't seen and are going around the circle imitating in stupid voices the cat or child or whatever it is supposed to be, so I step out front of the gym for a cigarette, and it's better outside, expansive, so I start walking and keep walking without purpose into the evening, knowing exactly where I'm going.

We walk in great droves, in a herd, from the city to the train yard to the trains. Beneath our feet is dirt, and cobblestone, and pavement. From village to village, carrying our books on our backs like bread. Carrying our bread in our sacks like books. The animal in me kicks in, recognising a feeling so ancient it's buried somewhere deep in our DNA. We move how goats are moved, in great mobs, to the slaughterhouse. If you travel far enough back, the genetic line of every living thing meets, one foot fall follows another somewhere in the double helix of us.

It's already dark by the time I arrive at Arnold's house. The blue paint's peeling around the windows and the streetlight casts its yellowed glow over the old Victorian making it a sour pickle green. It's taken me half an hour to walk here, or half a lifetime, and I've almost killed my whole pack of cigarettes. I know he doesn't live here anymore. Even though I've long since blocked his number, I still read along, keeping up from a distance, following what's happened online. He lost his job for an 'undisclosed reason', but it seems pretty clear something happened with one of the teens at his work. That he's now likely in some county prison for too short a time, but will be haunted by that registry for the rest of his life. I know if I told anyone this was my fault, they'd deny it, and even then, I'd know it would be true. So, I've decided not to talk about it. I could have guessed this was something he was capable of – that people who lock people in closets are capable of worse and I could have done something to stop it, simply by saying his name. Looking at that house again for the first time in years, I feel a crow pick at the carrion laid out on the flat road of my chest, some carcass that's been sitting there for years, unaddressed. The window of the room where I slept and the one where I was trapped make up the two eyes of an upside-down face.

I hope that kid's alright, even as I know he couldn't possibly be. Who was I when I lived here? Who was I when I fled? All the lights are off in the house. I can't tell if anyone's living in it, the value must have plummeted due to the circumstance, or maybe the realtor covered it up. I palm the empty pint of Wild Turkey in my hand thinking only to shatter it against the vinyl siding someone's slapped on the old building. I put every muscle I've got behind it, only for the bottle to slip out of my fingers so that in its revised trajectory, it crashes through the living room window, making a sudden gaping mouth in the side of the house, a black and empty tunnel for meat and speech to pass through. A lamp snaps on inside, and the mouth floods with light. I'm scared it will start speaking so I flee, quick as I can, back into the night I came from.

When I make it back to campus, I'm relieved to find the party's ended. Everyone's either paired off to make a mistake or split into small groups, dancing to music warping out from their phone speakers, or smoking weed on the quad beneath that same tree we all used to smoke under and complain about our lives. Possibly Janine is quietly crying in the dark behind the freshman dormitory, and I think *kindred*. Some boy with a distinguished jawline and his damp shirt unbuttoned all the way yells into his phone, assuring the person on the other end he misses them too and won't do anything stupid. Everyone's acting like children, acting even younger than we were when we went here.

Ericka comes over and we split my last cigarette on the bench where we used to judge people on their morning walk to class. This is the first chance we've had to talk and we return easily to that old practice. *Can you believe Alejandro's jacket? Did you hear what Kristina said at dinner? What psychopath is responsible for Jessica's hair?* They say they heard about what happened to me. I remember something I saw online about them losing their dad. *I heard about that*, I say. *Glad you flew across an ocean for this?* I ask. *Sure*, they reply, laughing. *The world is ending, why not stir up some bad memories?* I lean my head against their shoulder, and they rest their head on top of mine and it's like we never left and it's like we were never here at all. We were never here at all. *You're different*, they say, *colder seeming. Age made you cold.* Their curls are damp curtains in my face. *You're the same*, I say, *still fucking annoying.* We laugh and then we stop laughing. We stay like this until the field clears and we stumble back to sleep in our separate pasts – in twin beds in a dorm room designed by a man who got famous designing prisons. In the morning, we say our goodbyes as strangers.

One of the last things I do at the bookstore is curate a new section called *Dead Myths*. Lukas isn't into it. The idea is simple, the books can be about anything – ornithology guides, collected sex advice columns, the philosophy of time – with the only unifying factor being that they are texts once owned by people who have since died, who left some writing in the margins. On the first page of a volume of old Jewish folktales, there's a handwritten note that reads:

> Meredith,
> At the very least, I hope this will make you smile.
> I'm so sorry.
> > ~ yr dad
> > June, 1992

I build a little shrine in the back of the store to hold all the little markings we leave behind.

I hear he's dead the way everyone learns about their dead these days. The word *Remembering* appears next to your face, and then the comments come flooding in, everyone suddenly hyper-aware of your absence even though they haven't thought about you in years. Everyone trying to tastefully find out more information while sharing photos of you smiling.

I'm just scrolling, as one does, eating a burrito from a truck a few minutes' walk from campus, feeling deeply unimpressed by the quality of the chicken, when a photo of him comes up on my feed. He's young in the picture, about the same age he was when he first started coming over, the Yankees cap hasn't gotten filthy yet. He's holding up his two dogs, still small enough to have one under each arm. I smile before realising what this is. When I do, something in me falls open and keeps falling.

If we were living, I know he wouldn't remember; but now we're both gone, I'm betting he can't forget. We're sitting on the edge of my bed in front of my little television which casts its stalled glow over us like a blue gown. We were playing a game where two impossibly muscular men in tattered uniforms fight to the death, using their brutality as an excuse to touch, but now our avatars are paused and heaving. Something awful has happened at home, but of course he won't say what. His head's on my lap and it's a comfortable weight, I can feel him crying real quiet, the way he does, no tears, just an empty sort of shaking. I ask if he's okay, and he punches my leg one time, hard, and I feel it go numb. Then he tilts his face up and kisses me on the mouth for the first time.

His obituary, posted online by the local paper, is frustratingly vague and tells me nothing aside from the fact that it is, of course, a tragedy. In the time between learning he died and learning how, holed up in my dorm room, I witness every possible death in my mind: Edwin falling off a roof at work, Edwin's pickup run into the median by a drunk Winnebago, Edwin murdered in his bed by a jealous lover, Edwin eaten by his newly feral and starving dogs, a small wound in Edwin's foot unchecked grows septic, a clot in Edwin's thigh leads to a freak stroke, a bar fight gone awry, him swinging from a tree behind his mom's house, a wet stretch of pavement, a stray slab of concrete, a piano, a cigarette catches his blanket. When I do finally get down to the comment that gives more detail, it clarifies nothing, car accident, going north on I-95. Was he thrown from the blue pickup or did he die inside? Was it the other driver or was he too high to be driving? Did he mean to do it? Where does the fault lie? How could it not be mine?

Everything that follows has less taste. The colour of the world dulls to a sepia and never comes back.

When I arrive back at my apartment from the reunion, it doesn't feel like mine, my apartment, my body. And why would it? How many people have lived here since this building was constructed almost a hundred years ago – twenty families, twenty more? How many people have visited my body and never left? Alone in this city, I no longer get the same pleasure I once did walking, being invisible, becoming lost inside all these unstable environments. Invisibility can be another kind of violence. There are a hundred different apocalypses on the horizon, and what can I do? Everyone's either talking about it and not acting, or worse, not even talking, just going back to their salads and yoga classes and pashminas. And what can be done, really? I repost stuff online without comment. I go to work. I go to the demonstrations. I donate what money I can while staying comfortable. It's never enough. It's so hot in my apartment, I can't ever get a good night's sleep. The landlord has the heat on because technically it's winter, at least according to the calendar. I wake up each morning drenched in all the liquids my body refuses to process.

Even though I have almost no sex drive, I try to fill some of this emptiness with one last good mistake. I find an older man, a guy on Scruff, *Dad4Jung* (later, *Call me James*), with an expansive loft in Williamsburg. His pics make it seem like he discreetly owns several comfortable homes but doesn't want to appear showy about it. The apartment is beautiful as a room where old Hollywood careers were ended or began. His eyes are so blue they're almost white, two empty pieces of paper fixed on me as he fucks me on his cowhide rug. I leave my body for a moment and float above us, watching it all go down. It's not unsexy, this kind of discorporeal autoerotic pornography – somehow full and gone, stretched open and a thousand miles away. Once he's spent, he asks me to sleep over and I want to spend the whole night on that soft dead cow, only he insists I join him on his boutique memory foam mattress which holds onto the precise depression of my body. *Memory, holds, depression, body*. I keep finding meaning everywhere it isn't, while this guy, he keeps looking at me, rubbing my head and calling me his good son until he finally drifts off. This'll do just fine, I think. He has a beautiful library. Whole cases of untouched first editions of Marcuse, Fromm, and Fanon. I wonder what will happen to it after he dies? If he has a plan for all he's hoarded.

Alexandria burned and took with it centuries of knowledge. When we go, we do the same.

I'm up all night, thinking through tomorrow. This man sleeps as I map out my subway route and search my phone for a stop along my route to pause for gasoline. This man sleeps as wastewater's released into rivers, and people shiver in doorways. He's entirely unbothered, doesn't realise how easily I could rob him while he dreams. Nothing will touch him here in his money, in this little world he's built himself apart from the suffering of the world, but isn't that what we all eventually do? With money, if we get it? Even the best of us? Even if we think we'll be different? I text Lukas to let him know I won't be coming into work.

In the morning, I steal one of the man's fancy shirts and slip out before he wakes up. And there, in the early sunlight, on the corner of Union and Metropolitan, a goat is just standing there.

There's a family of plants called pyrophytes that have evolved to not just tolerate fire but require it. One species depends on wildfires to melt the wax around their seed pods; another for their seeds to germinate. Another species of plant only blooms in ash-fertilised soil, while another, eucalyptus, carries flammable sap that encourages wildfire spread in order to defend its habitat. All species adapt to their circumstance. All circumstance requires adaptation. What can't we learn from our natural world, from our nature? We turn away from the earth, forgetting we'll be interred in it. Sometimes fire is a language all on its own.

I imagine Dad, years from now, someplace with clean air. He lights my Yahrzeit beside his new family, all gathered around the flame slowly eating down its fat wick. The men have grown older and softer in their schoolhouse. They take turns cooking each other breakfast. They make their own soaps to sell in the town's farmers market. They maintain daily study. They cultivate a small patch of kale and tomatoes. It isn't paradise, of course, but it will do.

What follows death is the ritual of preparing the body for bureaucracy. The paperwork, the plot, the will, the story, the measurements, the casket, the service, the order. I remember everything.

I make a right onto Fifth Avenue and all my family is there. Thousands of us walking inside my body, each footstep so heavy we shatter concrete. Each square of sidewalk gapes like an open mouth behind us. Our sound empties the glass from every store window. We pause in the middle of the thin crowd which grows impossibly loud with all our voices. All our hands lift the canister over my head, all our senses flood with petroleum. So much was survived in order for me to end this line of thinking. So many of us are tired, and tried our best, and are ready to be gone. Tired of fleeing and of flight. They fill my lungs with salt as I turn my back on this country and turn back toward my countrymen and light a match.

1st Degree (superficial):

allergy planet

2nd Degree (patrial thickness):

soldier traffic

3rd Degree (full thickness):

ruined organ

Immolation:

bone mattress

The entire subway ride to midtown, I can't stop smiling in my expensive new shirt. Anyone who dares look at me receives back the unvarnished totality of my gaze, my new benevolent, unblinking eye. Unfettered and unfiltered. Maybe for the first time in my small life, I look deeply into each person's own deep pair of black pupils and think *sibling*, feel warmth spreading through the veins in my face. In each person, I see their whole person. I marvel how we each are meeting here, on this train below the city, somewhere between history and history. One by one they look at me, and one by one they glare, or shake their head, or pretend to look past me, or turn away – but each, in their own way, eventually smiles back.

ACKNOWLEDGEMENTS

An unending font of gratitude to everyone who has made my life and my writing possible. And especially deep gratitude to those who helped me realise these two things are inextricable. Micheal & Suzan (4always). To my family, blood and otherwise. To my writing family – so much love to Hieu, Danez, Cameron, Franny, Fatimah, Paul, Nate, Hanif, Kaveh, Jamila, Safia, Sarah, & Alison.

To those novelists who helped me imagine I could write a novel. And particularly the two folks I took fiction workshops with in graduate school a decade ago, Elizabeth McCracken and Alexander Chee – you two helped me believe I could play in y'alls sandbox, and showed me how big that sandbox actually is.

Gratitude to MacDowell, where I began this book in 2016, and to the Mesa Refuge where I put in some more work on it. Gratitude to that weird hotel in Petaluma, and every coffee shop and library where I muttered these sentences aloud to myself until they clicked home. Apologies to the students trying to study around me.

Big gratitude to Rita for your careful attention as my editor here and to Rob and Amanda and everyone at McSweeney's for getting this into the world, and deep gratitude to Dredhëza and everyone at Daunt.

To my colleague Kim at Stanford, and especially to my students who help me remember how art moves from, in, and upon the world. Thank you. Thank you. Thank you.